# FAMILY STYLE!

Glenn Boyd, the manager of the Mesa Flats Bank, came out of his office and looked around. His newly instituted security measures were in place. After the bank was robbed two weeks ago he vowed never to let it happen again. To that end he placed one uniformed, armed guard inside the bank, and two other guards, one dressed like a customer, one dressed like a teller. With three armed guards inside, and one on the roof, he felt sure that the bank was safe.

When the door opened he saw a family of four walk in: a father, mother, and two children, a boy and a girl. There were half a dozen other customers in the bank, as well, and it seemed as if business was back to normal. As he turned to go back into his office, though, he heard someone say, ''All right, this is a holdup, ladies and gents. If everyone does as they're told, no one will get hurt.''

Boyd closed his eyes and thought, Oh, no, not again!

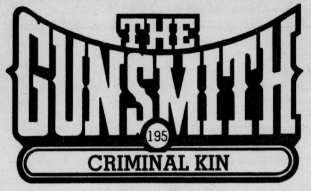

# THE GUNSMITH

### 195

## CRIMINAL KIN

## J. R. ROBERTS

**J**

JOVE BOOKS, NEW YORK

CRIMINAL KIN

A Jove Book / published by arrangement with
the author

PRINTING HISTORY
Jove edition /April 1998

All rights reserved.
Copyright © 1998 by Robert J. Randisi.
This book may not be reproduced in whole
or in part, by mimeograph or any other means,
without permission. For information address:
The Berkley Publishing Group, a member of Penguin Putnam Inc.,
200 Madison Avenue, New York, New York 10016.

The Penguin Putnam Inc. World Wide Web site address is
http://www.penguinputnam.com

ISBN: 0-515-12266-1

A JOVE BOOK®
Jove Books are published by
The Berkley Publishing Group, a member of Penguin Putnam Inc.,
200 Madison Avenue, New York, New York 10016.
Jove and the "J" design are trademarks belonging to
Jove Publications, Inc.

PRINTED IN THE UNITED STATES OF AMERICA

10  9  8  7  6  5  4  3  2  1

# THE GUNSMITH
## 195
### CRIMINAL KIN

# PROLOGUE

When the girl walked into his office Sheriff Frank Dobbs smiled at her. He'd never seen her before, but then he didn't know all the kids in town.

"What can I do for you today, little lady?" he asked.

The girl, who looked about ten, had yellow hair with a green bow in it and was carrying a large rag doll. She smiled back at the sheriff, took a gun out of the doll, and pointed it at him.

"Just sit quietly, Sheriff," she said, "and don't move until I tell you."

The gun looked ridiculous in the hands of the girl, but suddenly her eyes were flat and hard and she didn't look ten anymore. Sheriff Dobbs had no doubt that if he moved she would shoot him.

"That's good, Sheriff," she said. "You're taking me seriously."

"I always take a gun seriously," he said.

"By the way," she asked, "where's your gun belt?"

"It's in a desk drawer."

"That's a good place for it."

"What's this all about, anyway?" he asked.

"It's about you keeping quiet until I tell you different," she said. "If you force me to, I'll shoot you. Do you believe me?"

"Y-yes."

"That's good," she said. "That's real good."

"H-how long—"

"No more questions," she said.

The gun in her hand was a .45, too big for her, but she didn't seem to be having any trouble holding it steady in both hands.

The sheriff's mind was racing. This person in front of him looked like a little girl, pretty dress and ribbon in her hair, but she didn't look like any little girl he'd ever seen before. When he looked at her face now, he saw that she was older than he had first thought. Anybody not seeing her up close would say she was ten, maybe twelve at the oldest. Up close she looked older than that, but he'd be damned if she still didn't look like a kid.

What the hell was going on, he wondered.

When the mother, father, and two kids—a blond little girl and boy, both seemingly about ten or eleven—entered the bank of Langdon, Arizona, they drew no more attention than most families draw. The father was wearing a suit, the mother a dress and bonnet, and the children were well dressed, as if it were Sunday—but it wasn't. If it had been Sunday the bank wouldn't have been open, and then this nice little family of four couldn't have robbed it.

"Don't anybody move!" the man shouted, producing a pistol in his hand.

Now everyone looked at the family, as each member

was holding a gun in their hands, even the children.

"Watch the door!" the man shouted. The little boy nodded and moved confidently toward the door.

"Now," the man said, "if we don't get complete cooperation, people are going to die, understand?" He looked at one of the tellers, a man, and asked again, "Understand?"

"Y-yes, sir," the teller said.

"Good." He looked at the mother and daughter and said, "Watch everyone."

They nodded and pointed their guns at the bank patrons, of which there were five, three men and two women.

"Are you the head teller?" he asked the man.

"N-n-no—" the man stammered.

"I am."

He looked at the other teller, a woman in her thirties who was staring straight back at him with no sign of fear.

"You are?"

"That's right."

The man stared at the woman for a few moments, and she stared right back.

"Father," the woman with the bonnet said.

"All right, Mother," the man replied. To the head teller he said, "Empty the drawers."

"Into what?" she asked calmly.

"Find something!"

The male teller looked at her just as the door to the bank manager's office opened and a man came out.

"Mrs. Daly, what's going on?" he demanded.

"They're robbing the bank, Mr. Kaulfield."

"Who is?"

"This . . . family."

Andrew Kaulfield looked at the father, mother, and

two children, all holding guns, and said, "Preposterous."

"Shut him up, Mother," the man said.

The woman took three quick steps and slammed the barrel of her pistol against the man's head. Kaulfield, a big man with a lot of extra pounds on him, hit the floor like a sack of potatoes.

"He's shut, Father," the woman said.

The man turned back to the woman, Mrs. Daly.

"All right," he said, "let's get it done."

Mrs. Daly grabbed a money bag and held it open. She said to the male teller, "Come on, do it."

"How are we doing?" the father asked the boy at the door.

"We're okay."

He turned back to the tellers, who were now emptying the woman's drawer.

"Give me the bag," he said.

The woman looked at him.

"Don't you want what's in the vault?"

"Is it locked?" he asked.

"Well, yes—"

"And is he the only one who can open it?" he asked, indicating the unconscious bank manager.

"Yes, but—"

"Then we don't want it, you stupid bitch!" He grabbed the bag from her. She thought she could get him to fuss with the vault until somebody came along, perhaps looked inside, and raised the alarm.

"Mother?"

He handed her the bag, which she held open.

"Everybody drop your belongings in the bag," the man announced.

There was some hesitation.

"Don't make me say it again, or somebody will get shot."

If there had been another child in the bank he would have pointed his gun at the child. He'd done that before and it was very effective. There were no other children in the bank, though, so he took two steps and pointed his gun at one of the women.

"Everything in the bag."

People responded then and wallets, rings, and watches were dropped into the bag.

"Thank you, ladies and gentlemen," he said when the woman had closed the bag. "Our transaction for the day is finished."

Out of the corner of his eye he could see the female teller glaring at him.

"Now, when we go out the door is anyone going to get brave and try to run for help?"

There was no answer.

"I'll take that as a no," he said, even though he knew it was wrong. The woman was going to try to go for help. He could tell just by looking at her.

He looked at the little girl and then looked at the woman teller. The girl nodded. From that point on she kept her eyes on the woman.

"Let's go," the man said, and the woman with the bonnet and the money bag started for the door.

"Clear?" the man shouted.

"Clear," the boy at the door said, and he opened it.

The woman went out first, followed by the boy, then the man—watching the patrons—and the little girl—watching the female teller—backed out the door.

Just as they were clearing the door the female teller came out from behind her window and started for the door, herself. The little girl saw this clearly.

"She's coming," she said.

The man nodded and looked at the woman. As she approached the door her mouth was already opening to shout for help.

The man shot her in the open mouth.

•  •  •

"Jesus," the sheriff said, when he heard the shot. "What was that?"

"Sorry," the girl said, and shot him.

# ONE

When Clint rode into Langdon, Arizona, it was midday, and he was surprised at how quiet and sleepy the town looked. It was a midsize town, the kind that would usually have some hustle and bustle in the streets at this time of the day.

He rode directly to the livery, and a man came out to meet him.

"Where is everybody?" he asked as he handed Duke off to the man.

"Funeral."

"Funeral?" Clint asked. "Who died?"

"Mrs. Daly," the man said. "Bank teller."

"Was she sick?"

The man shook his head.

"Shot during a bank holdup."

"Too bad," Clint said. "Must have happened recently?"

The man nodded.

"Yesterday."

"What about the sheriff?" Clint asked. "Did he catch anyone?"

"No," the man said, "he got shot, too."

That stopped Clint. He had ridden into Langdon, Arizona, to see the sheriff, an old friend of his.

"Dead?"

"No," the liveryman said.

"Where is he?"

"He's over at Doc's."

"Take good care of my horse."

"I will."

"Thanks."

"Hey?"

On his way out, Clint turned.

"Yeah?"

"You a friend of the sheriff's?"

"That's right."

"He's, uh, a little upset."

"I'd think he would be, since he got shot trying to stop a holdup."

"That ain't exactly what happened."

Clint came all the way back into the stable and looked at the man.

"What do you mean, that ain't *exactly* what happened?" Clint asked.

"He got shot in his office."

"In the office?"

"That's right."

"By who?"

"One of the gang," the man said. "See, she went into the office to hold him there while the rest of the gang held up the bank."

"It was a woman?"

"Well . . . it was a female."

"A woman is a female."

"Yeah," the liveryman said, "but so's a little girl."

"I don't get you."

"Sheriff Dobbs," the man said, "was shot by a little girl."

"That's what he says?"

The man nodded.

"Well, maybe he was . . . delirious?"

"That's what some people thought, until the folks at the bank said that they were held up by a man, a woman . . . and two kids."

Clint frowned.

"Are you shining me on?"

"No, sir, mister, I ain't," the man said. "You ask him yourself."

"I will."

"I was just warning you that he was feeling, ya know, a little embarrassed."

If he had been shot by a little girl, Clint could see why he would be.

"I'll keep that in mind," Clint said. "Thanks."

"Don't mention it."

Clint started out again, then turned and asked, "How do I get to Doc's?"

# TWO

Clint went straight to the doctor's office without stopping at the hotel first. As he entered, a tall, very thin man with gray hair and a long jaw was coming out another door.

"Doctor?"

The doctor looked Clint up and down critically.

"You look healthy enough," he said.

"I am," Clint said. "I'm here to see Sheriff Dobbs."

"Are you a friend of his?"

"Yes."

"Because if you're not, he's in a foul mood," the doctor said.

"I am a friend," Clint said, "and he'll probably still be in a foul mood if what I heard is true."

"If you heard that he was shot by a child, you heard right. Let me tell him you're here. What's your name?"

"Clint Adams."

The man frowned.

10

"I know that name, don't I?"

"Maybe."

The doctor nodded and said, "I'll tell him you're here."

He went back through the same door, then stepped out again a few moments later.

"He says he'll see you. You can leave those things there, on the floor."

Clint put his rifle and saddlebags down.

"How is he?"

"If the bullet had been a little to the right . . . It missed his heart. He'll survive because he's lucky, and because I'm a good doctor."

"Sounds like a good combination," Clint said.

Clint stepped past the doctor, who closed the door behind him. Frank Dobbs was lying in one of three beds, the other two of which were empty. The doctor seemed to have himself a small hospital.

"Frank?"

Dobbs turned his head and looked at Clint.

"Go ahead, say it."

"Say what?"

"What everybody's thinking."

Clint looked around for a chair, found one, moved it next to the sheriff's bed and sat down.

"I don't think I can say anything until I hear from you what really happened," he said.

"Everybody knows—"

"Frank," Clint said, cutting him off, "I want to know what really happened, okay?"

Dobbs took a deep breath and said, "Okay, here it is . . ."

When Dobbs was finished Clint said, "Tell me about the little girl again."

"Well, when she walked in she looked like a little

girl, but when she took that gun out of the doll—''

''Wait a minute. She took the gun out of a doll? You didn't tell me that the first time.''

''I didn't?''

''No.''

''Well, it was this big rag doll, you know, and she let the doll drop and I was looking down the barrel of a forty-five.''

''A big gun for a kid.''

''She held it in both hands,'' Dobbs said, ''and she held it steady.''

''Did you really think she'd shoot you, at that time?''

''Clint,'' Dobbs said, ''I looked into her eyes and suddenly she wasn't such a kid anymore, you know? I think she and the others have done this before.''

''Tell me about the others.''

''I can only tell you what people told me,'' he said. ''If you want more you'll have to go to the people who were in the bank.''

''I will,'' Clint said, ''but tell me what you know.''

''A man, a woman, and two children—a boy and a girl—went into the bank, suddenly produced guns, and announced that it was a holdup.''

''Two more kids?''

Dobbs nodded.

''So your little girl was obviously sent to keep you from interfering.''

''Right.''

''What happened?''

''They clubbed the bank manager, emptied the tellers' cash drawers, took wallets and jewelry from the other people, and then shot Mrs. Daly on the way out.''

''Why did they shoot her?''

''Well, folks told me she was on her way to the door. She was a tough one, Clint, and I think she was going to call for help. She should have waited a little longer.''

"Who shot her?"

"From what I hear, the man."

"Anything else?"

"The people in the bank, they said the man and the woman called each other 'Father' and 'Mother.' "

Clint nodded.

"That was their way of making sure they didn't call each other by their real names. What about the kids? Did they call them anything?"

"Not that I was told."

"Okay, Frank," Clint said. His friend's eyelids were drooping. "You need to get some sleep."

"By the way," Dobbs said, his eyes closing, "it's nice to see you."

"Yeah," Clint said, "you, too. I only wish I'd gotten here a day sooner."

# THREE

Clint stopped to talk to the doctor one more time before he left the office.

"Doctor . . ."

"Merrick," the man said. "Is he asleep?"

"Yes."

"Good. He needs a lot of rest."

"Doctor, is there a deputy?"

"Yes," Merrick said. "His name's Paul Wilson."

"Is he experienced enough to do the job while the sheriff is laid up?"

"No," Merrick said, "he's a young man, very earnest and very serious, but not experienced at all."

"Has a posse gone out?"

"Yes, with Wilson in charge. They came back empty-handed."

"I'd better find this deputy and have a talk with him," Clint said.

"Given your, er, considerable reputation, perhaps the

14

town council would name you temporary sheriff—"

"Oh, I don't want the job," Clint said, shaking his head.

"Don't you want to help your friend?"

"As much as I can," Clint said, "but I'm not putting on a badge."

"Well, you must have your reasons."

"I do, Doctor," Clint said, "I do."

After Clint left the doctor's office, he went to one of Langdon's two hotels and checked in. After he dumped his rifle and saddlebags in the room, he went in search of a meal and settled on the hotel dining room. He was almost finished eating when a young man entered the room. He was tall, dark-haired, very serious-looking, intense. He had black hair and a pronounced Adam's apple, and he was wearing a badge. He looked around the room, spotted Clint, and came over.

"Are you Clint Adams?"

"I am."

"If you think you're gonna get my job, you're mistaken."

"And why would I want your job, Deputy?"

"You're . . . uh, friends with the sheriff, right?"

"That's right."

"Are you gonna try to get appointed sheriff until he's up and around?"

"Why would I do that?" Clint asked. "They have you for that job, don't they?"

"They do," the young man said, "but they don't want me."

"Then let them find someone to replace you."

"They are trying," the deputy said.

"Why don't you sit down and have some coffee?" Clint invited.

"I don't have much time," the deputy said.

"Surely enough for a cup of coffee."

The deputy sat without responding. Clint poured him a cup.

"Your name is Paul Wilson, isn't it?"

"That's right."

"Paul—can I call you that?"

The other man nodded.

"Paul, do you think you're ready to do the sheriff's job?"

"Well, sure . . . I mean, just until he gets back on his feet."

"Well, Frank hired you, right?"

"Yes, sir."

"Then he must have thought you were competent."

"Competent, yes," Wilson said, "but experienced, no. I admit I don't have much experience, but I've been a deputy for seven months."

"And you've learned things in that seven months, haven't you?"

"Yes, sir, I have."

"Well, then, stick to your guns, Deputy," Clint said. "Don't let them push you out."

"Have you seen the sheriff, Mr. Adams?"

"I spoke to him briefly."

"Did he . . . mention me?"

"No," Clint said, then added, "there wasn't time. We talked about what had happened to him, and the bank, and then he fell asleep."

"I see."

"Do you think he has confidence in you, Paul?"

"I hope he does."

"Have you talked with the people who were in the bank?"

"Yes."

"Would you take me to them so I could talk to them?" Clint asked.

"Why?"

"Well, like we just said," Clint said, "you don't have a lot of experience. Maybe I can find out something you missed."

"And you don't want the job?"

"I don't want your job or Frank's, Paul. I just want to help. All right?"

Wilson thought a moment, then said, "All right."

# FOUR

Outside Clint asked, "How far did you go with the posse?"

Wilson didn't look happy.

"Not as far as I wanted to," he said.

"Why?"

"The posse," he said, "wouldn't follow me because I'm . . . so young."

"You'd think they'd go as far as they had to. After all, it was their money."

"Well, that's another thing."

"What?"

"They only took the money from the cash drawers, and from each customer."

"Not the vault?"

"No."

"So that means they left most of the money behind."

"That's right."

Clint frowned.

"Well, that explains why the posse wouldn't go all out," Clint said. "Most of their money is probably still in the vault."

"Right."

"But that doesn't explain why the robbers were satisfied with so little."

"I don't know."

"Well, maybe they said something at the time," Clint said. "Maybe somebody will have heard something."

"I guess I should have asked," Wilson said. "I didn't think to ask that."

"It's okay," Clint said. "Don't worry about it."

"I . . . should talk to the sheriff," Wilson said. "Find out what he wants me to do."

"You haven't spoken to him since he got shot?"

"No."

"We'll go see him later," Clint said. "He was tired when I spoke to him."

"How did you get in to see him?" Wilson asked.

"I just heard about what happened when I rode in," Clint said. "I went right to the doctor's office."

"And he let you in?"

"Yes."

Wilson frowned.

"He wouldn't let me in."

Clint didn't say anything.

They walked awhile longer and Clint asked, "Where are we going?"

"You said you wanted to talk to the people who were in the bank when it was held up."

"So?"

"They're at the cemetery."

"Oh," Clint said, "right."

The funeral must have been just starting when he rode in. Now they were at the cemetery, watching the woman who was killed being lowered into the ground.

• • •

They were all Boot Hill. Some of them had different names, like this one: The Langdon Cemetery. Whatever they were called, though, they were all Boot Hill.

There was a crowd of people when they came within sight of the cemetery.

"Was this woman well-liked?" Clint asked.

"I don't think so," Wilson said. "I think a lot of people are just glad it wasn't them, and maybe feeling a little guilty about it."

Clint thought that was a very mature observation for a man so young. Maybe there was more to the deputy than met the eye. After all, Frank Dobbs was usually a good judge of people, why should it be any different with Paul Wilson?

When they got closer to the graveside Clint asked, "Are the people from the bank there?"

Wilson waited a moment then said, "Yeah, all of them. See the big heavy guy? That's the manager, Andrew Kaulfield. He got clubbed over the head during the robbery, doesn't know much after he came out of his office."

"And the others?"

"There were two tellers, Mrs. Daly and that skinny little guy next to Kaulfield. His name's Willis something, or something Willis, I forget."

"And the customers?"

"Looks like they're all there, too, and then some others."

As they looked on, the assemblage began to break up. Some of the people came their way.

"Introduce me to Kaulfield."

"He probably knows the least of all."

"Paul, doesn't the bank manager know the combination to the bank vault?"

"Well, sure."

"So why would the bank robbers knock unconscious the only man who could open it?"

Wilson scratched his head and said, "I don't know."

"Neither do I. Maybe Mr. Kaulfield has some ideas. Introduce me."

"All right."

As Kaulfield approached, the deputy called out to him by name. The man looked around, saw the deputy, and came over. The teller, for want of something better to do, came along as well.

"Deputy," Kaulfield said. "What can I do for you?"

"Mr. Kaulfield, this fella is a friend of the sheriff," Wilson said. "He wanted to meet you."

"Are you helping to chase down these robbers, Mister . . ."

"Adams," Clint said, "Clint Adams."

"Adams?" the banker repeated. "You mean, the Gunsmith?"

"Mr. Kaulfield, would you answer a few questions for me?"

"I will if you're going after those robbers."

"I'm just trying to be helpful here," Clint said.

"Walk with me back to the bank then, Mr. Adams, and we'll talk."

"All right."

Kaulfield looked at the teller.

"Willis."

"Yes?"

"Stop hanging on me."

"Yes, sir."

"You run ahead to the bank, I'll be there shortly."

"Yes, sir."

Clint wasn't surprised to see the little man actually run ahead of them.

"I'm gonna see if I can't get the posse back together

to go back out," Wilson said. "I also want to try to get in to see the sheriff."

"All right, Paul," Clint said.

Deputy Paul Wilson nodded to the bank manager and walked away.

"Let's walk," Kaulfield said. "He's a good lad, but he's got no experience."

"He'll get some," Clint said.

"Perhaps," Kaulfield said, "but not in time to help me or the bank."

"Mr. Kaulfield, I understand the robbers only took what was in the tellers' drawers."

"That's right," Kaulfield said, "they only got away with about fifteen hundred dollars of the bank's money. There was over a hundred thousand in the vault."

"Sir, why do you think they didn't try for the vault?" Clint asked.

"Well, for one thing, I was knocked unconscious, and no one else could have opened it."

"Sir, that's my question. Why would they knock out the bank manager, arguably the only one who might have been able to open the vault for them?"

"Well, I think there's only one possible reason for that, Mr. Adams."

"And what would that be, sir?"

"They never had any intention of trying to get into the vault."

"And why do you think that would be?"

"I can't imagine."

They reached the town limits and started walking down the main street.

"Maybe they were just after some easy money," Clint said.

"That could be."

"And maybe they thought getting into the vault would have taken too long."

"That makes them foolish," the bank manager said. "I mean, to risk their lives for so little."

"Maybe fifteen hundred is not so little to them," Clint said. "Especially if they've done this before."

"You think this is an experienced gang? Using children?"

"Who do you think they were?"

"Well, I thought they were probably a family who had fallen on hard times and decided to rob a bank. Then I heard about the other little girl who shot the sheriff."

"They could still be a family," Clint said, "but a family of bank robbers."

"What kind of family—what kind of parents teach their children to steal at gunpoint?" Kaulfield asked as they approached the bank.

"As you said, Mr. Kaulfield," Clint replied, "maybe a family that has fallen on hard times. May I come inside the bank and have a look?"

"Of course," Kaulfield said. "Come right in."

# FIVE

Inside the bank Clint had a quick look around. The teller, Willis, was behind his cage, looking jumpy. There were no customers and Clint commented on this.

"We're actually closed," Kaulfield said, "in honor of Mrs. Daly. Willis! The closed sign."

"Yes, sir."

"I see," Clint said.

"Willis," Kaulfield said, "tell Mr. Adams what happened yesterday."

The man was nervous and stammered through his explanation, but Clint got the idea. The young boy had been sent to the door to act as a lookout, and the "mother" had gone around to the customers, collecting their belongings.

"It was her, the 'mother,'" Kaulfield said, "who clubbed me to the floor."

"You're lucky you weren't more seriously hurt."

"I—I thought they were going to leave without hurt-

24

ing anyone,'' Willis said, ''but then Mrs. Daly went running for the door, and the man, the 'father,' he shot her.''

''And what about the little girl?''

''She warned that Mrs. Daly was coming.''

''And even the children were armed?'' Clint asked.

''Yes, sir,'' Willis said.

''Mr. Willis . . . did you get a good look at the robbers?''

''Oh, yes, sir.''

''And tell me, were the children really children?''

''Excuse me?''

''What I mean is, could they have been adults—uh, short adults—dressed as children?''

''Well,'' Willis said, screwing up his face as he concentrated, ''no, I don't think so. I think they were definitely children.''

''All right,'' Clint said, ''then maybe they were older than they looked?''

''I suppose that's a possibility.''

''Oh, Willis,'' Kaulfield said, ''you're not being very helpful, are you?''

''Sir—''

''He's doing the best he can, Mr. Kaulfield,'' Clint said. He looked at the teller. ''Thank you, Mr. Willis.''

''It's just Willis, sir,'' the man said.

''Well, Mr. Adams, if that's all, we do have some work to do.''

''Yes,'' Clint said, ''I think I'm finished here. Thank you for your time, gentlemen.''

Kaulfield went to the door, let Clint out, and then locked it. Clint stood in front of the bank for a few moments, looking up and down the street. From where he was he couldn't see the sheriff's office. He went in search of it.

# SIX

He found the office empty and stepped inside, anyway.
It was not far from the bank so the sheriff certainly
would have heard the shot. So would the little girl,
which was probably why she shot Dobbs. Maybe those
were her instructions, to shoot him at the first sign of
trouble.

Clint was about to leave the office when Deputy Wilson came in, looking agitated.

"What th—oh, it's you," Wilson said, recognizing
him.

"What's wrong?"

Wilson slammed the door.

"I can't get anyone to go back out with me," he said.

"Why?"

"Oh, they all say they have businesses to run, and
that their money is still safe in the bank, but I know the
real reason. They don't have any confidence in me. They
won't follow me."

"Did you talk to the sheriff?" Clint asked.

"Not yet."

"Why don't we go over and see if he's awake," Clint suggested. "You can tell him your problem."

"I'd just like to see how he is," Wilson said. "Sheriff Dobbs, he means a lot to me."

"Okay, Paul," Clint said, "let's go see how he is."

When they walked into the office the doctor looked up from his desk.

"He's awake," he said. "You can go in."

"Thank you, Doc."

Clint opened the door, let Wilson go in first, and then went in after him.

Dobbs looked at them from the bed.

"Hey, kid," he said. "How're ya doin'?"

"I was gonna ask you that," Wilson said, taking off his hat and walking to the bed. "How are you, Frank?"

"Oh, I'm doin' fine," Dobbs said. "Doc got the bullet out and says I'll be fine. I see you met Clint, huh?"

"Yeah, he, uh, talked with Mr. Kaulfield."

"He did, huh?"

"Just trying to be helpful," Clint said.

"What are you doing here, kid?" Dobbs asked. "Why ain't you out with a posse?"

"I was, Frank," Wilson said, "but they all wanted to come back."

"You should have made them stay out there, Paul."

"I tried, Frank," Wilson said, almost whining. "They wouldn't listen to me. They don't respect me."

"You got to make them respect you, kid," Dobbs said. "They ain't gonna give you respect if you don't earn it."

"I know, Frank . . ." Wilson said, fingering his hat.

"You got to get them to go back out, Paul."

"They all say their money is still safe. The robbers only got away with a little of it."

"Fifteen hundred," Clint said.

Dobbs tried to whistle but his lips were too dry.

"Not so little," he said. "You still got to go after them, Paul."

"All right," Wilson said, "I'll try again, Frank."

"Good lad. Why don't you wait outside while I talk to Clint, huh?"

"Sure, Frank. I'm glad you're gonna be all right."

"That makes two of us, kid."

Dobbs smiled at Wilson and waited for the deputy to leave.

"Clint—"

"Frank, don't say it!"

"You got to help him," Dobbs said. "He can't do it alone."

"Frank—"

"I'm not askin' you to put on a badge," Dobbs said, "just back him up."

"And ride with the posse?"

"They won't follow him without you."

"Frank, this isn't my problem—"

"Who are you kiddin'? You're already workin' on it."

"It's a flaw I have," Clint said. "I was just trying to be helpful."

"So keep tryin' to be helpful."

"My idea of being helpful is to ask questions, Frank," Clint said. "Not ride out with a posse."

"Let me ask you this," Dobbs said. "Ain't you curious about this? About a family—a father, a mother, and three kids—robbing a bank, shooting me, and killing a teller?"

Clint rubbed his jaw.

"It is curious, isn't it?"

"Damned right it is," Dobbs said. "The more I think about it, the more I know the girl who shot me looked twelve, but she was older."

"Was she a kid, Frank? Could she have been an adult dressed like a kid?"

"No," Dobbs said, shaking his head, "she was a kid, but she was no twelve-year-old."

"Maybe they just dress them young," Clint said. "And who says they're a family?"

"What?"

"Maybe they're not related."

"The adults called each other 'Mother' and 'Father.' At least, that's what I was told."

"That was just to keep from calling each other by their real names," Clint said. "There's no proof that those kids are really theirs."

"So they're just using kids to help rob banks? Why?" Dobbs asked.

"It throws everybody off balance, doesn't it?" Clint asked. "Weren't you thrown?"

"I never suspected a thing," Dobbs said, shaking his head. "She had the drop on me before I knew what was going on. I feel damn foolish about that."

"Why?" Clint asked. "How were you supposed to know?"

"Would a kid ever get the drop on you, Clint?"

"You know," Clint said, "I've thought about that some. A kid is probably the *only* one who could ever get the drop on me, Frank—at least, until today."

"Yeah, well," Dobbs said, "at least you didn't have to learn that lesson the hard way. Look, Clint, I need your help."

"Frank—"

"The kid needs your help."

"The town doesn't seem to care about the money," Clint said.

"I care!" Dobbs said. He lifted his head as he said it and then hissed in pain and grabbed his chest.

"Take it easy, Frank."

Dobbs took a moment to catch his breath.

"That little girl almost killed me, Clint," he said. "In fact, I'm surprised she didn't. Her hands didn't shake a lick while she was holding that gun on me."

"Are you thinking she left you alive on purpose?"

"I don't see how she missed killin' me," he said. "She could have shot straighter—"

"Or again," Clint finished.

"Right."

So there was another interesting question.

"What do you say, Clint?"

After just a moment he said, "All right, Frank. As a favor to you, and because I am curious about these people."

"Attaboy! Thanks a lot. Go and tell Paul."

"All right." Clint also wanted to send out a telegram before he went with Wilson to try to round up the posse again. "You take care of yourself, and do what the doctor says, huh?"

"Sure," Dobbs said, "and you catch that bastard and his . . . his family, or whatever you want to call it."

"I'll do my best, Frank."


Wilson was waiting outside, rather than in the doctor's office.

"What did he say?" he asked.

"He wants me to help you," Clint said. "Do you want my help, Paul?"

"Well, sure," Wilson said. "I could learn a lot from you, Mr. Adams."

"Well," Clint said, "the first thing you're going to learn is to call me Clint."

"All right, Clint."

"And the second thing is how to round up a posse. You take me around to all the men who rode with you the first time."

"All right."

"But first I want to go to the telegraph office," Clint said.

"What for?"

"I've got a friend of mine who might have some information about this . . . this family of bank robbers. It would help us if we knew something about them before we took off after them."

# SEVEN

Clint followed Deputy Wilson to the telegraph office, where he sent a telegram to his friend Rick Hartman in Labyrinth, Texas. Rick had more contacts all over the country than anyone Clint knew. If anyone had information about the family of bank robbers, or if anyone could find any, it was him.

"What if he don't answer today?" Wilson asked as they left the telegraph office.

"He will," Clint said. "He'll answer very soon, and while we're waiting we'll go see those posse members of yours."

Each of the posse members were town merchants, and as Clint and Wilson entered their establishments they were all ready with their excuses—until Wilson introduced Clint by name.

"You're Adams?" Eldon Campbell, the owner of the general store, asked.

"That's right."

"If you don't mind me asking, sir," Campbell said, "why are you getting involved in this? This isn't even your town."

"Sheriff Dobbs is a friend of mine," Clint said, "and I don't take kindly to having my friends shot."

"Well," Campbell said, "that's reason enough, I guess."

"It should be reason enough for you, too, Mr. Campbell," Clint said.

"Well, the sheriff is no great friend of mine, Adams—" Campbell started.

"I was talking about having your bank robbed, and a teller killed," Clint said.

"Well, now, my money was in the bank vault, wasn't it? And it still is."

"That shouldn't matter," Clint said. "It's still your bank, Mr. Campbell, and who's to say some of that money that was taken wasn't yours?"

"It wasn't—"

"That's up to Mr. Kaulfield to say," Clint said, "and he's doing an inventory right now. How do you think he'll feel when he finds out you wouldn't ride out with the posse?"

"I rode out—"

"Well," Clint said, "the posse is going out again in two hours—and bring enough supplies to stay out a few nights."

"A few nights—"

"If necessary," Clint said. "Now, if you'll excuse us, we have other posse members to see."

Outside, Wilson asked, "Do you think he'll show up?"

"He'll show up," Clint said. "He doesn't want to be on the bad side of the bank manager. Now let's go see the others."

• • •

They went and saw all ten men who had ridden out with Wilson the day before, and two extra, so that if everyone showed up they'd have fourteen men in the posse.

Clint and Wilson went back to the sheriff's office to check the rifles and shotguns in the gun racks, and that's where the clerk from the telegraph office found them.

"Here's your answer, Mr. Adams."

"Thanks."

"Say," the man said, "do you fellas mind if I ride out with your posse?"

"Harry—" Wilson started, but Clint stopped him.

"Is there anyone else in town who can operate the key, Harry?" he asked.

"No, not really, but I want to help—"

"While we're out there," Clint said, "we might have to send a telegram back here. What's going to happen if you're out there with us?"

"Guess I didn't think of that."

"You'll do us more good here."

"I guess I will at that," the man said. Clint thought he looked a little relieved. "Guess I'll get back to work."

As the man went out the door Wilson asked, "What does your friend say?"

Clint scanned the telegram, then looked at Wilson.

"Nothing."

"Nothing?"

"He never heard of a gang like this," Clint said, dropping the telegram on the desk.

"That surprises you?"

"Yes," Clint said. Then he added, "No. If there was anything to know, Rick would know it. They must be new. In fact, this might have been their first job—except they seem to have been so organized. Everything went so well.''

''Until one of them shot Mrs. Daly.''

''Right,'' Clint said, ''and that made the girl shoot Frank—except that Frank thinks she could have killed him easily.''

''You mean he thinks she let him live?''

''Well,'' Clint said, ''there was no guarantee he'd live from that wound, but she could have shot him through the heart.''

''Then why didn't she?''

''I guess that's the question, isn't it?''

# EIGHT

"Clint?" Wilson said a few moments later.

"Yes?"

"Does it make sense to go out today?" the deputy asked. "We won't get real far before we have to stop for the night."

"It makes sense to get these men on horses and out of town as soon as we can, Paul," Clint said. "Before they change their minds."

"I guess you're right."

"Which direction did the gang go when they left?" Clint asked.

"Folks said they saw them ride out to the west."

"On horses?"

"Well, yeah . . ."

"All of them?"

"I guess . . ."

"Even the kids? They had their own horses?"

Wilson scratched his head.

"Find out, will you?" Clint said. "Go out and ask around."

"Okay."

"Also find out about the girl who shot the sheriff. Did she have her own horse? Did they ride back here to pick her up, or did she ride to join up with them by the bank? There must have been people in the street who saw something that day."

"Okay, Clint."

As Wilson went to the door, it suddenly opened and a man stepped in. He was a well-dressed man in his fifties with the look of someone who was used to people going around him, which Wilson did, saying, "Afternoon, Mayor."

"Deputy. Is this fella Clint Adams, by any chance?" the man asked Wilson.

"That's him, sir."

"Thank you, Deputy."

Wilson completed his walk around the mayor and left. The mayor closed the door behind him.

"Mr. Adams? I'm Mayor Harlan J. Coben."

"Glad to meet you, Mr. Mayor. What can I do for you?"

"Well, as I understand it, you and the young deputy are going to take the posse out again."

"That's right."

"Don't you think the trail is a little old by now?" the man asked.

"Actually, I don't," Clint said. "Two adults and three children will leave a trail."

"I see what you mean," Coben said. "Well, then, let me get to the point. We—and I speak with the full support of the town council, here—would like you to take over for the sheriff until he gets back on his feet."

"You've got the deputy for that," Clint said.

"As you can see our deputy is young—he's a fine

young man, but he's very young, and inexperienced.''

"Well, I'm afraid he's all you've got, Mayor," Clint said, "because I'm not putting on a badge."

"You haven't heard my offer of wages," the mayor said.

"It wouldn't matter."

"Twice what Sheriff Dobbs was getting," the mayor said, confident that this would change Clint's mind. "It's the least we can do for a man of your—"

"Why don't you just increase the deputy's wages while he's in charge?"

"Frankly, he's not worth what you or what Dobbs was worth."

"I'm sorry, Mayor," Clint said. "My answer is still no."

"But—but you're riding with the posse."

"As a volunteer."

"But we're willing to pay you."

"I'm doing it as a favor to my friend, Frank Dobbs."

"But if you're wearing the badge the men will follow," Coben said. "Mark my words, after a few hours in the saddle these men will be ready to come back to town. They won't stay for the deputy, but if you were in charge—"

"I'll be there, Mayor," Clint said, "maybe that will be enough."

"Sir—"

"I'm sorry," Clint said, "but you have my answer."

The mayor walked to the door with a puzzled look on his face. At the door he stopped and tried again.

"Three times the wages?"

Clint smiled and said, "Sorry."

The mayor shook his head and left.

# NINE

Clint decided to go to the doctor's office and give Frank Dobbs an update. When he entered he was surprised that the doctor was not there. He entered the room where Dobbs still occupied a bed.

"Where's the doc?" he asked.

"He had an emergency," Dobbs said, still lying flat on his back. "Somebody's havin' a baby. How are things goin', Clint?"

Clint pulled a chair over and sat down.

"The posse should be ready to go within the hour," he said.

"They agreed?"

Clint nodded. "Two more than Paul had yesterday."

"That's two more that will decide to come back after a few hours."

Clint rubbed his nose and said, "That might not be such a bad idea."

"What do you mean?"

"I mean Paul and I may be able to travel faster on our own."

"When did you think of that?"

"Just now, as a matter of fact."

"So then why take a posse?"

Clint shrugged.

"Just to inconvenience them."

Dobbs laughed.

"In the days when you were a sheriff, you must have dealt with a lot of this."

"I did," Clint said. "It's a thankless job that you do, Frank. You know that, don't you?"

"Sure I do," Dobbs said. "If I wasn't lying here with a bullet hole in my chest, everybody in town would be demanding to know why I didn't stop that robbery."

"And why you weren't out trying to find that gang."

"Oh," Dobbs said, "if I wasn't laid up that's what I'd be doin'. I want to find that girl who shot me."

"I'll find her for you."

"And bring her back here."

"Where else would I bring her?"

"Any other news?"

"A bit."

First Clint told him about the telegram he'd gotten from Rick regarding the gang.

"Not a word?" Dobbs asked.

"Nothing."

Dobbs remembered Clint's friend Rick.

"I thought he had connections."

"He does," Clint said. "The gang must be new."

"This girl was in control, Clint," Dobbs said. "I don't think this was the first time she did this."

"Maybe not," Clint said. "Rick will keep his ears open."

"Anything else going on?"

"Well, yeah," Clint said. "Your mayor offered me

your job—just while you were recuperating, of course."

"What did you tell him?"

"I told him no."

"Did he offer you more money than me?"

Clint hesitated, then said, "Yes."

"Then it must have confused him when you turned him down," Dobbs said. "Our mayor thinks money buys you everything, just because it bought him the election."

"Well, it didn't buy me."

"He's not gonna fire the kid, is he?"

"Not that I know of," Clint said. "I told him I'd be going along with the posse as a volunteer."

"When you could have been paid for it?" Dobbs laughed. "That's really got to puzzle him."

"He did look kind of confused when he left your office," Clint said.

"Clint," Dobbs said, "if the posse quits on you, will you continue on?"

"Me and Paul both, Frank," Clint said. "Traveling the way they are, they'll leave a trail."

"What if they don't travel the way they were when they left here?"

"Well," Clint said, "I guess that would make them very, very smart."

# TEN

Stan Wilkins knocked on the door of the hotel room and entered without waiting for a reply. The girl was sitting on the bed, and she turned her head to look at him as he entered. Wilkins marveled again at how young she looked, at how easily she was able to convince people she was four or five years younger than the eighteen she really was. Of course, the fact that she was only about five feet tall helped.

Holly was the first one Wilkins had found, and consequently they had a "special" relationship. It was his relationship with Holly that gave him the idea to put the gang together. Of course, his "wife" Beth—or "Mother" as she was called when they were holding up banks—had to be convinced, but when he'd explained it all to her she had come around.

The other two "kids" were sixteen and fifteen, but they were easily dressed to look younger. It was a great plan, and it had worked perfectly in Langdon, where they'd tested it. The job had gone off without a hitch, until that bitch of a teller had come out from behind her cage with her big mouth open. Well, he'd shut it for her, sure enough.

Holly had simply done what she'd been told to do. At the first sign of trouble pull the trigger and shoot the sheriff. Of all of them, Holly was the one he trusted.

Now, as he entered the room and closed the door behind him, he felt his erection growing inside his pants. Beth had wanted to know why Holly deserved her own room instead of sharing it with the other two kids, but Stan had told her that she was older than them, eighteen. She needed some privacy.

If Beth only knew why Stan wanted Holly to have her own room . . . but with any luck, she'd never find out.

Beth was out shopping now, although she had instructions not to spend too much of the money.

Holly got up off the bed now and came toward him. They didn't usually have to talk to communicate. She knew what he wanted.

She was still wearing the little girl's dress, and when she peeled it off and dropped it to the floor and stood there naked he nearly came in his pants. Good God, it was erotic watching that transformation. Anyone seeing her in that dress would never suspect the perfect little body that was beneath it. She had small, perfectly shaped breasts and flawless skin. Her tummy was flat, her hips slender, and although she had a beautiful little butt on her, the little girl's dress often hid it.

She came to him now and undid his belt buckle. He'd left his gun in the room he shared with Beth. He wouldn't need it here.

She tugged his pants down around his ankles, and then his underwear. His erection jutted out at her, red and pulsing. She licked her lips, then closed her eyes and ran her tongue up and down the length of him. He'd had to teach her how to do this, but she had been a quick student because she loved it so much.

"Mmmm," she moaned, sucking him wetly, slurping and if he were a candy cane. Her head began to bob up and down, quicker, as her lips and tongue slid over him, and she sucked him in. She slid her hands around to cup his buttocks tightly as her head bobbed faster and faster until finally he had to pry her away from him before he finished in her mouth.

She knew what he wanted, even then. She went to the bed and got on her back. He finished undressing, kicking his clothes away, hastily pulling his shirt over his head without unbuttoning.

He went to the bed and sat beside her. He ran his hand over her perfect body as she closed her eyes. His erection was throbbing, but he didn't want to rush. He pinched her nipples and squeezed her breasts. He ran his hand down over her belly and into her blond pubic hair, probed her with his middle finger until it was inside of her. She grew wet right away, wiggled her butt, and said, "Please . . ."

He straddled her, spread her legs, and then eased himself into her. He wanted to pound into her like a bull, but he was trying to control himself. Still, he couldn't take as long as he wanted because Beth wouldn't be shopping all afternoon.

He moved in and out of her slowly for a few moments, and then couldn't help himself. He started to slam into her, grunting with the effort, reaching down and cupping her buttocks, pulling her to him, squashing her with his much bigger body and then biting his lip to keep from bellowing when he exploded inside of her.

He rolled off of her then, breathing hard from the effort. He wiped himself off on the bedsheet, then stood up, gathered his clothes and put them on.

"We'll be in the dining room for dinner," he said to her, "at six. Come down with the others."

"All right."

He nodded, then went to the door and left, walking down to his own room. His legs were trembling and he was still hard. He wanted her again, but he was going to have to wait. But so was she, the little slut. She enjoyed it just as much as he did. She'd been a virgin when he first took her, although she'd been eighteen even then, but she was far from a virgin now. She knew exactly what she was doing, and loved every minute of it.

If only Beth was a *little* bit like that . . .

# ELEVEN

After Stan Wilkins left, Holly Burke brought her knees up to her chest and rolled onto her side. Tears slid down her cheeks as she cried silently for fear that Wilkins might hear her.

When he'd poked a finger inside of her, her whispered ''Please . . .'' had not been a plea for even more intimate contact. It had escaped her lips inadvertently and, luckily for her, had been misconstrued by Wilkins as a plea for sex.

Holly had, indeed, been a virgin when Stan Wilkins found her. In the beginning he had been kind to her, buying her clothes, and food, and giving her a place to stay, and that first night that he had come to her bed she had decided—very quickly—to let him do what he wanted to, out of gratitude.

After that, however, he came more frequently, and she dared not refuse him. In fact, as he taught her how to do the things he wanted, she had been able to convince him that she liked it—which was, of course, untrue.

By this time he had brought the other two children into the fold and had already explained the plan that he had for them to rob banks. The other two children—Sally and Ben—were sneak thieves anyway, picking people's pockets when they could, and moving on to bank robbing was exciting to them.

Holly wanted nothing more than to get away from Wilkins, but she knew she couldn't. One time she had thought to tell Beth what was going on, but Beth was mean and that would probably make her meaner.

And when she thought about it, Stan Wilkins had never been mean to her. She had given into him willingly in the beginning, so how could she reject him later on, when his visits became more frequent?

Now all she wanted to do was to try to put some money aside from their robberies, until she had enough saved to be able to leave. She could have run away now, but he'd find her. She needed money to be able to avoid him.

Still, they had taken almost two thousand dollars from that bank in Langdon, and he had not given her—or the other two children—any of it.

Holly knew she had two things in her favor. She was Wilkins's favorite. At least, she didn't *think* he was doing the same things with Sally that he was doing with her. After all, Sally was only sixteen.

Second, she had convinced Wilkins that he could trust her. Nothing convinced him more of that than the fact that she had shot the sheriff in Langdon.

Holly had always been a good shot and she felt pretty certain that she had not fatally shot the man. When Wilkins read in the newspaper that the sheriff had been shot, that was good enough for him. He didn't even care that the man hadn't died.

"You'll learn," he had told Holly, "to make a more

fatal shot in time. You did fine for your first time.''

Holly heard someone walking in the hall and she knew it was Beth, coming back from shopping. What would she have done if she'd caught Wilkins coming out of her room? For a moment Holly wished that had happened, but in the next moment she knew that Beth—as angry as she might have been at Wilkins—probably would have taken her anger out on her.

For now, she thought, hugging herself tightly and feeling Wilkins's leavings on her thighs, it was probably better this way.

# TWELVE

Beth walked into their room and glared at Wilkins. They were not married, although they were registered as husband and wife. They had been together for several years, however, first in the East working together to con people out of their money, and now in the West as—of all things—bank robbers. How she had let him talk her into this she'd never know.

Wilkins was reclining on the bed as she entered. He came to his feet and kissed her cheek.

"Hi, sweets. What did you buy?"

"Have you been here the whole time?" she demanded.

"Of course I have."

"Didn't sneak down the hall to that little slut's room?"

"Honey," Wilkins said, "how many times have I got to tell you that you've got Holly figured all wrong."

"She'd like you to dump me and take up with her,

that's what I get,'' Beth said, dumping her purchases on their bed.

Wilkins took hold of her arms and looked into her eyes.

"That's nonsense, sweetie," he said. "Nobody could take your place."

"You'd better believe that," she said, poking him in the chest. "No one else would put up with you."

"Don't you think I know that?" he asked, pulling her to him. He had washed up and changed clothes since coming from Holly's room. There was no way Beth could smell Holly on him.

"Why don't we put these things over here," he said, taking her packages off the bed and putting them on a chair, "so we can use the bed for something else, hmm?"

"Stan—"

He pulled her toward the bed and down onto it, then pushed her down onto her back. Beth was thirty-two and starting to show the wear and tear of the years, but she still had a good body, and bright, blond hair. Wilkins was still hard from being with Holly, from thinking about Holly, and as Beth put her hand on him and felt his hardness she smiled, sure it was for her.

Wilkins liked sex with Beth—he *loved* it with Holly, but still liked and enjoyed it with Beth. He undressed her slowly, and she yanked at his belt and freed his erection so she could stroke it. Wilkins was thirty-seven and felt great satisfaction with himself that he could have sex with eighteen-year-old Holly and then, half an hour later, again with Beth.

He didn't drag it out with Beth, though, didn't spend time admiring her body and running his hands over it. He peeled her out of her clothes, straddled her, and plunged into her. She wrapped her legs around him and raked his back with her nails—something Holly had been specifically warned against doing—while he rammed himself into her again and again until they were both grunting and crying out, and he made no effort this time to be quiet because he didn't care who heard him. In fact, he *wanted* Holly to hear him all the way down the hall, wanted her to be jealous of him and Beth together.

The time would come, he knew, when he would replace Beth with Holly, but not just yet. There were still a lot of things Holly had to learn first . . . and not all of them were in bed.

And then, of course, there was always Sally, who, in two years, would be eighteen, herself.

He smiled as he continued to pound into Beth. Holly to replace Beth, and then Sally to replace Holly. . . .

Down the hall, in a room between the one Beth and Wilkins were in and the one Holly was in, Ben Spencer and Sally Tanner listened to the sounds the two adults were making next door. Earlier, they had listened to the sounds Wilkins and Holly had made through the other wall.

Sally, at sixteen, blond and pretty in a gawky sort of way, was a virgin, but found herself thinking more and more about boys recently—and Ben in particular. Ben was a year younger than her, but they were both small people. That was why Wilkins had taken them in. She had learned that the year between them was not all that much, really. She wondered if she could get Ben interested in her . . . as a woman.

Sitting on the other bed, Ben, also blond—which made it easy to believe that he was brother to Sally and Holly—was not thinking about girls. He was thinking about how it had felt to hold a gun on those people in the bank. He was wondering how it would have felt if he had been the one to shoot the woman.

At fifteen Ben had not yet begun to show an interest in girls—least of all Sally, with whom he was pretending to be brother and sister.

"Ben?"

"Yeah?"

"What do you think Beth would do if she found out about Stan and Holly?"

Ben looked at her and laughed.

"She'd probably kill them both."

Sally's eyes widened.

"She'd kill Stan?"

"Well," he said, "she'd kill Holly, for sure."

"That would ruin everything."

"Yeah, it might."

"So why is he doing it?" Sally asked. "Why is he taking that chance?"

Ben gave her a superior look and said, "Because he's a man, and men can do whatever they want."

# THIRTEEN

"They're outside," Deputy Paul Wilson said as he entered the office.

Clint, even though he had been alone in the office for some time, had decided not to sit behind the sheriff's desk. It was not his place to do so, but Wilson's.

"Let them wait awhile," Clint said. "It'll do them some good."

Wilson shrugged and looked around the office.

"Sit down, Paul."

He started to get a chair from a corner, but Clint stopped him.

"Sit behind the desk."

"Me?"

"You're in charge."

"Aw, Clint," Wilson said, "you and me, we know who's in charge—"

"You're officially in charge," Clint said. "Go on, sit."

Wilson hesitated, then shrugged and went around to sit behind the desk.

"When we go out there," Clint said, "you're going to give the instructions and the orders."

"They won't listen to me."

"Sure they will."

"Only 'cause you're behind me."

"In the beginning," Clint said, "but from then on you're going to have to earn their trust."

"And what if I can't?" Wilson asked. "What if after a few hours they decide to turn back?"

"Then we'll keep going."

"Just the two of us?"

Clint nodded.

"We're after a man, a woman, and three children, aren't we?"

"Yeah," Wilson said, "children with guns."

"Still," Clint said, "we'll keep going, and we'll bring them back, and maybe that will earn you a measure of respect in this town."

"Yeah," the deputy said, "maybe."

"Where's your horse?" Clint asked.

"At the livery."

"Mine, too," Clint said. "Maybe we should go and saddle up."

They both got up and went out the front door. The men were milling about, most of them having gotten down off their horses, all of them either wearing a gun or holding a rifle or, in some cases, both.

"Hey, Adams," one of them shouted, "when are we gonna get going?"

"Ask the deputy," Clint called back. "He's in charge."

The men looked at each other while they pondered that one, and then one of them finally called out, "Hey, how about it, Deputy? When do we get movin'?"

"Clint and I have to saddle our horses," Wilson called back. "We'll meet you back here, and we'll get moving within the next half hour."

A grumble went up, but beyond that nobody complained—at least not until Clint and the deputy were out of earshot.

In the livery, as they saddled their horses, Wilson asked, "Does the sheriff know what we're doing?"

"He does."

"Did he ask you to look after me?"

"He asked me to help you," Clint said. "There's a difference, Paul."

"I guess."

"Look," Clint said, "you've got to make up your mind about something. Either you want my help or you don't."

"I do, but—"

"Then don't feel bad about getting it," Clint said, cutting him off. "You're going to come out of this with some experience, Paul. That's what you should be thinking, here, and that's all."

"I am thinking about that," Wilson said, "but there's something else I want."

"What?"

"I want to bring that son of a bitch back here," Wilson said. "That man who put a bank robbery gang together from women and children."

"Well," Clint said, "when we catch up to them we'll find out just how much that woman and those children are being led, won't we?"

They rode their horses back to the jail, and when the other men saw them coming they all mounted up.

"Where we headed?" one of them asked.

"Same direction," Wilson said. He and Clint had discussed it.

"We covered that area yesterday," one of the posse said. "Shouldn't we try someplace else?"

"That's the direction they were seen going in," Wilson said.

"But—"

"Do any of you read sign?" Clint asked.

There was a chorus of nos and some shrugs.

"Well, I do," Clint said. "I should be able to tell whether or not we're on the right track. If we need to change direction, I'll let the deputy know."

Dean Winslow, the owner of the gun shop, asked, "So you're along as tracker?"

"That's right."

"You ain't wearin' a badge?"

"I'm a volunteer," Clint said, "just like the rest of you."

"Volunteer," someone said, "like hell." But Clint gave Wilson a warning glance to ignore the remark, and the young deputy rode to the head of the posse and led them out of town.

# FOURTEEN

While Clint had been a lot of things in his time, he'd never actually been a tracker. He had, however, learned to read the stories that the ground could tell about who had passed this way or that.

They rode west for a couple of hours before some of the posse members started complaining.

"How can he tell which way they went since yesterday?" one of them complained out loud.

"You got me," another said. "To me the ground looks too hard to tell anything."

"You want to say something to them?" Wilson asked Clint as they rode ahead of the other men.

"No," Clint said, "let them squawk. Are we going to come to the next town soon?"

Wilson nodded and said, "Bisbee's comin' up in about half an hour."

"That's when we'll find something out."

"Why do you say that?"

"Figure it out," Clint said. "A man and a woman and three children—two of them girls—on horseback, that's going to attract a lot of attention, don't you think?"

"Well . . . yeah."

"I figure they had to change their mode of transportation soon after they left Langdon."

Wilson frowned.

"Meaning what?"

"Meaning traveling more the way a normal family would travel."

Wilson thought a moment, then said, "In a wagon."

"Right," Clint said, "a wagon, a buckboard, something along those lines. If they were going to do that they would have had to stash a wagon somewhere."

"They could have put it anywhere."

"Not if they wanted to be sure it would still be there when they got back," Clint said.

"They could have left somebody to guard it."

"They could have," Clint agreed, "but let's hope they didn't. Let's hope they left it in the closest town to Langdon."

"Bisbee."

"Right," Clint said, "and if they did that, somebody will be able to tell us."

"And if they didn't?" Wilson asked. "Or if nobody knows anything?"

"Well, then," Clint said, "we'll have to come up with a better idea, won't we?"

As the posse rode into Bisbee they complained some more.

"This is silly," one of them said. "We rode all this way just to come to Bisbee?"

Bisbee was much smaller than Langdon, and this many men riding into town attracted a lot of attention.

"We'll leave the horses at the livery," Clint said to Wilson. "You'd better tell the men to get themselves some rooms—and double and triple up where they can."

"Right."

Wilson gave those instructions, and the men muttered about it amongst themselves.

"Jesus," one of them said, "I could get home before nightfall and sleep in my own bed."

Clint kept Duke outside the livery, waiting for all the others to make arrangements for their horses. The liveryman was thrilled to have that much business.

As the posse members all walked away from the livery, Clint rode Duke inside and dismounted. Paul Wilson was still there, waiting.

"That's a fine-lookin' animal you got there, mister," the liveryman said to Clint.

"Thank you."

"I'll take good care of him."

Clint gave Wilson a look which told the young man to take the lead.

"Can I ask your name, friend?" Wilson asked.

"You kin ask," the man said. He was in his late fifties with gray hair and gray stubble. "Guess I'd answer you, seeing as how you're the law and all."

"What's your name, then?"

"Last name's Bonner," the man said, "but folks around here call me Bonny. You be needin' my given name?"

"No," Wilson said, "Bonny's fine. Bonny, I'd like to ask you if you've seen or done business with a family recently?"

"What kind of family?"

"Mother, father, three kids."

"What kind of kids?"

"Two girls and a boy."

"Pretty gals?"

"I guess . . ." Wilson said, starting to lose his patience.

"The kids could be anywhere from thirteen to eighteen, Bonny," Clint said. "You seen anyone like this lately?"

"Sure have."

"When?" Wilson asked.

"Well," Bonny said, "they come in here a few days ago and asked if they could leave their buckboard here. Since that's my business I said sure."

"What then?" the deputy asked.

"Then they rented some horses and rode off."

"And when did they come back?"

"Yesterday," Bonny said. "Seemed in an all-fired hurry. Wanted their buckboard back, give me back my horses, and off they went."

"Did you see what direction they went in?" Wilson asked, growing excited.

"No."

Wilson frowned.

"No idea?"

"None."

Wilson looked at Clint.

"Guess I ain't been real helpful, huh?" Bonny asked.

"Sure you have, Bonny," Clint said. "It just would have been more helpful if you'd seen what direction they were going."

"Didn't see," Bonny said, "but I heard somethin'."

"Like what?" Clint asked.

"Like two of them kids talkin'," he said. "The boy and one of the girls."

"And what did they say?"

"They was excited."

"Why's that?"

" 'Cause they said they ain't never been to Mexico before."

"Mexico," Wilson said, looking at Clint, who gave him a look that said they shouldn't discuss it here.

"Thanks very much, Bonny," Clint said.

"Hey," the older man said, "thankee for the business, and I'll tend to your horse real good."

"I know you will," Clint said.

"Clint—" Wilson said, but Clint shushed him again.

# FIFTEEN

Before they left the stable, Clint asked the liveryman to show him where he had kept the buckboard.

"What for?"

"I'd just like to see."

The man shrugged and took them out back.

"It was there."

Clint walked over to the spot behind the stable that the man indicated.

"Did they leave right away?" he asked, looking at the ground.

"Huh?"

Clint looked at the man.

"I asked if they left right away when they came for the buckboard, or did they stay in town?"

"Oh," the man said, "uh, I guess they stayed overnight."

"Which means they left this morning."

The man shrugged and said, "I guess so. The buckboard was gone this morning when I got here.''

Clint nodded, then said to the man, ''Thanks. Now can you show us the horses they rented?''

''Sure . . . I guess . . .''

He took them to the corral out back and pointed the horses out, then said, ''I think that spotted sorrel, too, but I ain't sure.''

Clint looked at Wilson, who nodded to him.

''Okay,'' Clint said to Bonny, ''thanks. Let's go, Paul.''

''Now we've got a lead on them going to Mexico,'' Wilson said, outside the livery.

''If the liveryman is telling the truth,'' Clint pointed out.

''Why would he lie?''

''Paul, people lie,'' Clint said, ''and you don't always know why.''

''So what do you do?''

''You proceed with caution,'' Clint said. ''Do you think if they came here after robbing the bank that they'd stay the night?''

''Don't make sense, does it?'' the deputy asked.

''No, it doesn't. It also doesn't make sense for them to go to Mexico.''

''Why not? It's a good place to hide out.''

''From what we know,'' Clint said, ''they've hit one bank, yours. It was probably a test run. Now they're going to want to start hitting other banks, and they can't do that in Mexico. They want to do it here.''

''And then hide out in Mexico?''

''Maybe, but that wouldn't be until after they've hit quite a few banks and built up a bankroll.''

''So . . . how do we find out if he's lying?''

''Did you see the tracks the buckboard made?''

''Uh . . . no.''

"One of the rear wheels, the back right one, has got a distinctive chip in it. It'll leave tracks like no other wheel."

"So then you'll be able to follow it?"

Clint nodded.

"As long as they're traveling over a road that'll hold their tracks. We should be able to tell what direction they're going in, anyway. What about those horses, Paul? Did you get a description of the horses they were riding?"

"That spotted sorrel," Wilson said, "somebody described it."

"That's good," Clint said. "At least we know they really were here."

As they approached the hotel Wilson asked, "Do you think they paid the liveryman off?"

"It's possible," Clint said.

"Then he could have lied about them having a buckboard."

Clint looked at him.

"Now you're learning," Clint said. "But I don't think he did."

"Why not?"

"That would require imagination on his part," Clint said, "and I don't think he's got any. I think if he's lying, it's just to try and throw us off, send us in the wrong direction."

"I hope you're right," Wilson said. "I don't want to be following a buckboard with a distinctive wheel if it's bein' driven by somebody else."

"I feel the same way, Paul," Clint said, "but this feels right to me."

"Guess that's what you mean by experience."

"Well," Clint said, "we'll find out pretty quick if my experience is pointing us in the right direction, or the wrong one."

# SIXTEEN

When they reached the hotel they discovered that all but one of the rooms had been taken.

"We're a small hotel," the clerk apologized, "and a posse just came into town—"

"I know," Wilson said, "it's my posse. I'm Deputy Wilson, from Langdon. We had a bank robbery a couple of days ago."

"Was anyone hurt?"

"They killed a woman, a teller," Wilson said. "And they shot our sheriff."

"Sheriff Dobbs?"

"That's right."

"Is he dead?"

"No," Wilson said, "he'll be all right."

"Did you have a family staying here recently?" Clint asked. "Parents, three kids—two girls and a boy?"

"No," the clerk said, shaking his head, "I'd remember that. We're not all that busy, you know? We, uh, appreciate your business, Deputy.''

"We'll take the remaining room,'' Clint said.

"Yes, sir.''

The clerk handed them the key.

"Hope you don't mind sharing a room,'' Clint said, as they walked up the stairs.

"Hell, no,'' Wilson said. "I can ask you questions all night now.''

"That'll be fun.''


Clint and Wilson found the other posse members in the saloon, some at the bar, others scattered around at tables. There were a few townspeople in the place, but mostly it was taken up by the posse.

"You the deputy?'' the bartender asked. He was a big man with a thick neck and heavy shoulders and arms, most of it muscle but some of it going to fat.

"That's what the badge says.''

"These your boys?''

"They're my posse, yeah.''

"Well, they say you're paying for the drinks.''

"That what they said?''

"Uh-huh.''

Wilson looked at Clint, who kept quiet.

"Well, when it comes time to pay up,'' Wilson told the bartender, "you tell them they're on their own.''

"I'll tell them that right now,'' the bartender said, "before they get too liquored up.''

"Give us a couple of beers, first,'' Clint said, and then added, "I'm buying.''

The bartender set them up and then came out from behind the bar to collect his money from the posse members.

One of the posse came up to Wilson and complained.

"Can't even buy us a few drinks, Deputy?''

Wilson turned and said, "Mr. Krebs, when we get back to town you talk with Mr. Kaulfield at the bank. I'm sure he'd be willing to pay you back for whatever you spent while with the posse."

"Why ain't the town of Langdon payin'?"

"That you'd have to take up with the mayor."

"This means we got to pay for our own hotel room?"

"That's what it means."

"Shoot . . ." the man said, and drifted away.

Clint looked around the room and saw all the posse men reluctantly dipping into their pockets to pay for their own drinks. Nobody seemed to be giving the big bartender any back talk.

"After this," Clint said, "we'd better go see the local law."

"Think he knows something?" Wilson asked.

"Probably not," Clint said, "but it's a courtesy to check in with him."

At that moment a man walked into the saloon and Clint saw the badge on his shirt.

"Or maybe we won't have to," he said, with a nod in the lawman's direction.

Wilson said, "Huh?" and turned to look.

The sheriff of Bisbee came walking over to them, a man of medium height, in his forties, who had the relaxed air about him of a man who had worn his badge for a while.

"Deputy," he said.

"Sheriff," Wilson said. "We were about to come to your office."

"Appears I saved you the trouble," the sheriff said. "Saw your boys come ridin' in here earlier, thought I'd wait around for their boss. That you?"

"It's me," Wilson said. "Deputy Paul Wilson, from Langdon."

"Langdon," the man said. "That's Frank Dobbs's town, isn't it?"

"That's right," Wilson said. "I'm Sheriff Dobbs's deputy."

"Where's Frank?"

"Laid up," Wilson said. "We had a bank robbery two days ago and Frank got shot."

"Bad?"

"Bullet in the chest," the deputy said, "but the doctor says he'll make it."

"Well, that's good," the other man said. "My name's Fenton, Andy Fenton. Been sheriff here for about fourteen years or so."

"Long time," Wilson said.

Fenton laughed shortly and said, "Yeah, too long. What brings you to Bisbee?"

"Following a trail."

"You mean I got me some bank robbers in my town?"

"Had, is more like it," Clint said. "Seems like they left some of their belongings here with your liveryman, then came back to get them."

"That so?" Fenton asked, looking at Clint. "And who might you be?"

"My name's Clint Adams, Sheriff," Clint replied.

"Adams?" It was clear he knew the name. "What are you doing with this posse?"

"Frank Dobbs is a friend of mine," Clint said. "I volunteered."

"Shoot," the sheriff said, looking at Wilson, "you got the Gunsmith ridin' with you, what do you need with all these storekeepers?"

"This is a duly appointed posse, Sheriff," Wilson said. "All these men had money in the bank."

Fenton took a moment to look around the room at the posse members.

"How long you boys figure on bein' in town?" he asked them.

"Just overnight," Wilson said. "We'll get an early start come morning."

Fenton nodded, then looked around again.

"Well, some of these boys look kind of thirsty," he said. "I got no beef with you as long as they behave. If they don't, I'll have to take it up with you . . . Deputy."

"They'll behave, Sheriff," the deputy said. "You got my guarantee."

Fenton nodded and said, "Fine," and left without further word.

"Should we have told him about the liveryman?"

"Told him what?"

"That the man might have been paid off by the bank robbers."

"How do we know the sheriff wasn't paid off, too?" Clint asked.

"But—but he's the sheriff."

"Lots of men use their badges to make extra money, Paul," Clint said.

"I'll bet you didn't."

"No, I didn't."

"And not Frank, or I'd know about it."

Clint doubted that, but he said, "No, not Frank, but I've known a lot of men who have. I've learned not to trust anybody just because they're wearing a badge."

Wilson looked dumbfounded.

"God, if you can't trust a lawman, who can you trust?"

"Yourself, kid," Clint said, picking up his beer, "always trust yourself."

# SEVENTEEN

The posse stayed in the saloon for most of the night, and eventually a couple of girls started working the floor. Clint watched the men closely. The sheriff was right in his assessment of them. Most of them were storekeepers, and a lot of them were married and away from their wives for the first time in a long time. They were the ones who were grabbing at the girls, trying to pull them into their laps, flirting with them.

Clint and Wilson were still standing at the bar, and he turned to the young deputy.

"You better close this down before it gets out of hand," he said. "We have to be up early in the morning. Most of these men are acting like they're on vacation."

Wilson looked around and said, "Yeah, you're right."

"Don't make a big announcement," Clint suggested, "just go around to each table and tell them it's time to go."

Wilson put his beer on the bar and said, "All right."

Clint watched as the deputy did as he'd suggested. He moved from table to table, leaned over and spoke to each man in turn. Some of them gave him the kind of look a child gives an adult when they think the adult is trying to ruin their fun. A few of them looked over at the bar, saw Clint standing there, and then nodded, got up and left. Eventually, most of the posse was gone, except for one table with three men sitting at it. Clint recognized the gun shop owner, Dean Winslow, but not the other two men. They were laughing and enjoying themselves, and Winslow had his arm around the waist of one of the girls, a pretty brunette with pale skin and soft-looking breasts, holding her close. As Wilson approached them it was clear that the girl was trying to get loose, but Winslow was strong, and was holding her fast.

With most of the men gone Clint could hear the conversation across the room.

"Time to turn in, boys," Wilson said.

Winslow looked up at him, and Clint could see, even from where he was standing, that the man was drunk.

"Look who's callin' us boys," he said to the other men, and then started laughing.

"Mister," the girl said, "you're hurtin' me—"

"Relax, sweetie," Winslow said, "I ain't even begun to pay attention to you. We're gonna go upstairs in a little while, you and me, and get better acquainted."

"I don't think so," the girl said. "I don't do that."

"Who are you kiddin'?" Winslow said. "All saloon girls are whores."

"Well, not me," she said. She gave Wilson a pleading look. "Can you make him let me go?"

Clint watched the proceedings with interest. This was one of the situations where the deputy was going to learn something.

"Let her go, Winslow," he said. "It's time to turn in. We got an early start tomorrow."

"You got an early start tomorrow, Deputy," the gun shop owner said, "not me. I ain't goin' any further than this. In fact, I might stick around Bisbee for a while and get to know this little gal a whole lot better."

"I don't think she wants to get to know you, Mr. Winslow," Wilson said.

"No," the girl said, "I don't."

"See? You'd best let her loose now."

"Why don't you go back to your friend at the bar, Deputy, and leave us be?"

Wilson looked at the other two men.

"You men better get back to the hotel."

They exchanged a glance between them, then pushed their chairs back to leave.

"Hey, hey, hey," Winslow shouted to them, "where ya goin'? You gonna let this pup tell you what to do?"

The men paused, but Wilson said, "Keep going," and they did.

"Hey—"

"Winslow!" the deputy shouted.

The man looked startled and turned his attention to Wilson.

"Let the girl go . . . now!"

Winslow stared at the deputy for the longest time, then released the girl, who wasted no time putting some space between them.

"You talk big, Deputy," Winslow said, "when you got the Gunsmith backing you up."

"He's at the bar, Winslow, and he's not coming over here," Wilson said. "Now, if you've got something to say to me, say it, or get your ass out of that chair and over to the hotel."

Winslow needed a few minutes to make up his mind, and the deputy was giving them to him. That was the only thing Clint would have done differently. He wouldn't have given the man time to think.

Finally, the man stood up and faced the deputy.

"You know," he said, "I don't only sell guns, I can use one, too."

"And that's why I wanted you on this posse," Wilson said, "but if you intend to go back to Langdon, then do it. We'll try to get along without you."

"Oh, I'm goin', all right," Winslow said. "I got better things to do then follow some young idiot who doesn't know where he's goin'."

With that Winslow stormed out of the saloon, and Wilson returned to the bar and picked up his beer. Clint noticed that his hand was shaking.

"You did good," Clint told him.

"Did I?" Wilson asked. "I was hoping he couldn't see me shaking."

"He didn't," Clint said. "He was too busy shaking, himself."

Clint slapped the younger man on the back and they drank together.

# EIGHTEEN

In the morning half of the men decided to follow Dean Winslow back to Langdon. Clint wondered if the man had stayed up all night talking to them.

While they all gathered at the livery stable and collected their horses, Paul Wilson pulled Clint over to one side.

"How do I get them to stay?"

"You don't."

"But . . . you and Frank said I had to make them respect me."

"Well, you could shoot Dean Winslow."

"I don't want to shoot Mr. Winslow."

"Then you can give him a beating."

Wilson frowned.

"I don't know if I want to do that, either. I don't even know if I could."

"Well, you backed him down last night. Unfortunately, no one else was around to see it."

"Then what do I do?"

"Just let him go, Paul," Clint said, "and let whoever wants to go with him go. When we come back with the bank robbers, people will remember who turned back."

"And then they'll respect me for not turning back, even though I lost half my posse."

"Right."

"So far."

Clint thought the young man was right. As they watched a belligerent Winslow ride off with half the posse, Clint thought they'd probably lose some more men along the way, especially if they did have to go all the way to Mexico—which he still doubted.

The rest of the men gathered around and looked toward Clint and Wilson.

"Better talk to them," Clint said.

Wilson stepped forward into a semicircle formed by the posse members' horses.

"We have a definite lead on how the gang was traveling when they left here, men," he said. "Clint is going to be able to track them, we hope long enough to determine which direction they're headed."

"We heard they was headed for New Mexico," one of the men said.

"We ain't goin' all the way to New Mexico, are we?" another asked. "I got a business to run."

Wilson ignored the second man and looked at the first.

"Who told you that, Mr. Claymore?"

Claymore, who ran the feed and grain in Langdon, said, "The liveryman came into the saloon last night and told some of us that's what he heard them sayin'."

Wilson looked at Clint, who came forward. It seemed as if Bonny was getting his stories mixed up. First he was saying Mexico, and now New Mexico, which was east, not west of them.

"We're not all that sure we should be believing the

liveryman,'' he said aloud. He was sure that the man himself, Bonny, could hear from inside the stable. ''We're going to have to depend on the robbers' tracks to tell us where they're going.''

''If it is New Mexico, or Mexico, or California,'' Wilson added, ''that's where I'm going. I hope you'll all come along.''

''Seems a long way to go for fifteen hundred dollars or so,'' Claymore said.

''You're forgetting, Mr. Claymore,'' Wilson said, ''that Mrs. Daly was killed, and the sherriff was shot.''

''You'll forgive me for sayin' so, Deputy,'' Claymore said, ''but getting shot is a hazard of the sheriff's job, and he knows that.''

''And what about Mrs. Daly?'' Wilson asked. ''Is getting shot a hazard of a teller's job, these days?''

Claymore looked around at the other men and said, ''I don't know about the rest of you, but I never did really like Mrs. Daly all that much.''

''Not enough to get killed for,'' one man said.

''Or ride all the way to New Mexico for,'' another man said.

Clint frowned, looking the remaining six men over, then he grabbed Wilson's arm and backed away from the group with him.

''Let them all go,'' he said to the young deputy.

''What?''

''Tell them to go home,'' Clint said. ''They'll be bitching and moaning the whole way, they'll probably slow us down, and eventually they'll turn back, anyway. This way you're taking the responsibility of bringing this gang in upon yourself.''

''But . . . just the two of us?''

''Don't worry,'' Clint said. ''We can handle it.''

Wilson stared at Clint for a few moments, then

shrugged and—still dubious—walked back to the men and told them to go home.

"Clint and I will handle this ourselves," Wilson said. "It's my job."

"You don't have to tell me twice," Claymore said. He wheeled his horse around. "You boys comin'?"

He rode out of town with four men following him. One man stayed behind. He was young, probably younger than Wilson, and he stared down at Clint and the deputy.

"What about you, Newly?" Wilson asked.

"If you fellas don't mind," Newly said, "I got no business to run, and I'd just as soon ride along with you. I ain't never seen New Mexico."

"We may not end up in New Mexico, Newly," Clint said. "Or Mexico."

The young man shrugged and said, "Wherever we end up, I ain't never seen it."

Wilson looked at Clint.

"Can you use that gun you're wearing?" Clint asked.

"Some," Newly said. "I'm better with my rifle."

Clint looked at Wilson.

"Well, you were worried that there would only be two of us," Clint said. "Now there's three."

# NINETEEN

They picked up the wagon tracks from behind the livery and followed them out of town. There was not that much traffic on the main street of Bisbee, and the ruts from the wheels were still there.

"See the distinctive track?" Clint asked, giving both of them a lesson in tracking.

They both nodded.

They followed the tracks out of town.

"They've got two horses pulling the buckboard," Clint said, dismounting and getting down on one knee, "and it looks like one is trailing along behind. Can't tell if it's being ridden or led."

"I can't tell anything," Newly said.

"It takes a while to get the hang of it," Clint said.

"They're headin' west, then?" Newly asked.

"They were, up to here," Clint said. "We'll have to see if they change direction."

Clint got up and mounted Duke again.

"We'll lose the tracks eventually," he said. "Let's follow 'em as long as we have 'em and see where they lead us."

"We're with you," Wilson said. "Lead on."

They followed the tracks for half a day and then the tracks petered out. The road got harder, and around them it was grassy. The ground was not conducive to holding tracks this long.

"What do we do now?" Wilson asked.

"Let's camp and think it over," Clint said. "I could use some coffee."

They divided the chores. Clint saw to the horses, because Duke probably would have taken a piece out of the two young men. Newly went for the firewood, and Wilson prepared the coffeepot. When the fire was going and the pot was on it, Clint passed out some beef jerky.

"What's your guess, Clint?" Wilson asked.

"My guess is they'll want to put some distance between them and Langdon before they hit another bank. Things didn't go quite as smooth as they would have wanted."

" 'Cause they shot two people," Newly said.

"Right, Newly," Clint said, "and one of those people died, and the other was a lawman, so they'll want to keep going."

"How far?" Wilson asked.

"California, maybe," Clint said. "There are plenty of banks in California."

Newly had not been privy to the earlier conversations of Clint and Wilson, so they brought him up to date on what they were thinking.

"So, this might not be a family, and the kids might not be kids?"

"Oh, they're kids," Clint said, "just not as young as they'd like us to think."

"Why the dress-up, then?" Newly asked.

"To put people off their guard long enough for them to get the drop on them," Clint said. "Even if there's a bank guard, he's not going to suspect someone he thinks is a young girl, and he'll be shocked when she sticks a gun in his ribs."

"And even more shocked if she pulls the trigger," Newly said.

"Right," Wilson said.

"I've been thinking about that," Clint said. "It was the man who pulled the trigger in the bank, but one of the girls who shot the sheriff."

"So?" Wilson asked.

"He must have had a lot of confidence in that girl to give her that job."

"You'd think he'd have at least one more adult along, maybe a man," Newly said, "for that kind of job."

"Maybe he doesn't want another adult along," Clint said. "And maybe he doesn't want another man along. Maybe he's got all of these people right where he wants them, and wants to keep it that way."

"You think maybe those kids are doin' what they're doin' against their will?" Wilson asked.

"I'm thinking maybe they don't know what their will is," Clint said. "I'm thinking they might need someone to show them they can have minds of their own."

"I guess we could show 'em," Newly said, and then added, "if they don't start shootin'."

# TWENTY

"When are we going to pull another robbery?" Beth
asked.

She was lying in the crook of Wilkins's arm and had
startled him from his thoughts of Holly, in another room
in the hotel. This was their third hotel since the robbery
in Langdon, and each time he'd managed to get Holly's
room far enough away from his and Beth's so that, even
if Beth was in their room, she wouldn't hear them.

Beth had been insistent about sex on this night, so
Wilkins had satisfied her, and was now waiting for her
to go to sleep so he could go down the hall to Holly's
room.

But she was awake . . .

"Huh?" he said. "Sorry, babe. You woke me up. I
was driftin' off."

"I asked when we were going to do another bank?"
she repeated.

"Not for a while," he said. "We shot a lawman in

Langdon. There's probably still a posse out lookin' for us.''

''How far will they follow us?'' she asked.

''Probably not far,'' he said, ''but I want to make sure. Now, why don't you go to sleep, huh? I want to get an early start in the morning.''

''All right,'' she said, rolling over onto her side, ''but I'm anxious to start making all that money you've been talking about.''

''Oh, don't worry,'' he said, pleased that she had rolled off of him, ''we're gonna make some money.''

''We had money back East,'' she murmured sleepily. ''Maybe we should go back there . . . get rid of these kids and go back East . . . maybe . . .''

Wilkins listened intently and waited for her breathing to indicate that she was asleep.

Go back East? Not a chance. The simple fact that she was talking that way was an indication that maybe they had come to the end of the line together. They wanted different things now. She wanted to go back East and he wanted to stay in the West, rob banks, and he wanted Holly.

He had to admit that he was starting to feel strongly about Holly—maybe too strongly. The other two—Sally and Ben—he could let them loose, and they'd be able to take care of themselves. Even Beth would land on her feet, but Holly . . . she was more fragile than they were. She needed him to look after her, and that's what he intended to do.

What he hadn't intended to do was fall asleep, but soon his breathing was as measured as Beth's, and he slept, dreaming about Holly.

# TWENTY-ONE

They had a choice now.

"Nevada," Clint said, "or California?"

They were camped for the night and sitting around the fire. They were several days out of Bisbee, and soon they'd have to make up their minds which border to head for.

"I can go either way," Newly said. "Like I said before, I ain't never been nowhere."

"I'm thinkin' California," Wilson said.

"Tell me why?" Clint asked.

Wilson shrugged, searched for an explanation, then simply said, "It *sounds* better. You know, more prosperous, more settled . . . more banks."

Clint nodded and said, "That makes sense. Banks are what they're looking for, after all."

"I got a question," Newly said.

"Ask it," Clint replied.

"What if they doubled back on us?" he asked. "What

83

if they are headed for Mexico, or New Mexico . . . or what if they went north?''

"I've got a friend who's got ears all over the country," Clint said. "The minute there's another robbery by a family of bank robbers, we'll find out about it from him."

"How?" Newly asked.

"We'll stop wherever there's a telegraph office and I'll contact him. If we are headed in the wrong direction we'll find out, and we'll head in the right one, then. Eventually, we'll catch up to them."

"Now," Newly said, "it don't matter to me how long it takes. I ain't got no one waitin' for me back in Langdon, but ain't you two got lives to get back to?"

"This is my life," Wilson said. "I don't have anyone in Langdon, either, but I owe the people something."

"The same people that left you in Bisbee and went back?" Newly asked.

"I owe Mr. Kaulfield, the banker," Wilson said, "and I owe Sheriff Frank Dobbs. I ain't stoppin' until we catch them."

"What about you, Clint?"

"Hey, right now my life is riding around, seeing different places, different towns and states—and I'm doing that, ain't I? But like Paul says, I also owe this to Frank. He's a friend of mine, and somebody shot him down without a thought. I want to catch them, too."

"One of the girls shot him, right?" Newly asked.

"That's right," Clint said, "but she was sent by the man. It's him I want."

Newly looked at both men and asked, "Is this posse stuff supposed to get so personal?"

Clint looked back at Newly and said, "You know what? You get first watch."

* * *

The watches were easy with three people, two and a half to three hours each. Clint took the last one and was awakened for it by Wilson.

"It's quiet," the deputy said.

"I thought it would be."

"Then why set up watches?"

"It's a habit you should get into when you're tracking someone," Clint said, rolling out of his blanket. "Newly was right about one thing."

"What?" Wilson asked, while wrapping himself in his blanket.

"Sometimes they will double back on you," Clint said. "It pays to be careful."

"Mmmm," Wilson mumbled, and then he was asleep.

Clint went to the fire and hoped that the two young men had left some coffee. There was half a pot, so apparently they hadn't drunk much, if any. He poured himself a cup and then sat down by the fire, being careful not to look into it and ruin his night vision.

Newly's last question had hit home. When you were a part of a posse you weren't supposed to let it become personal. It was personal to Clint because Dobbs was a friend of his; personal to Wilson because he had something to prove. Newly was really just along for the ride, because he had never been anywhere and this was a good opportunity for him.

Whatever the reason, the three of them were committed to tracking down this "family" of bank robbers, and with that kind of commitment, Clint was sure they would . . . eventually.

# TWENTY-TWO

They crossed into California the next day, and the first town they came to was called Buxton. It was small but had all the amenities: hotel, saloon, livery, and even a telegraph office.

"Are we stopping here?" Wilson asked.

"If it's okay with you," Clint said, always prepared to defer to the young man's "lawman" status—but the deputy never "pulled rank" on Clint, figuring that the older man knew what he was doing. "I think we should rest the horses, ask some questions, and I should send a telegram to Rick and see if he's found out anything."

"That suits me," Newly said. "We can get some real food."

"Oh, yeah," Clint said, smiling, "that, too."

Within the first hour they had dropped their horses off at the livery, checked into the hotel—a separate room for each of them—gone to the saloon for a drink, and asked the bartender for a good place to eat. He directed them to a small café, where they had all gone and ordered steaks.

The meal was over now and Clint had ordered another pot of coffee.

"Not for me," Newly said. "I never was much of a coffee drinker. I'm gonna look round the town some."

"Don't ask any questions," Clint warned him. "Let's leave that to the deputy, all right?"

"Sure," Newly said with a wave, "whatever you say. See you later at the hotel, or the saloon."

Newly left and Clint poured a cup of coffee for himself and for Deputy Wilson.

"I appreciate what you're doin' in front of Newly," Wilson said.

"What am I doing?"

"You know," Wilson said, "makin' like it's me who's in charge."

"You are in charge, Paul," Clint said. "All I do is make suggestions."

"Yeah," Wilson said, "and I'm smart enough to take them, huh?"

"That's part of being a smart lawman," Clint said.

"Well, when should I start asking these questions of mine?"

"When we finish here I'll go and send the telegram and you can ask some questions around town. Why don't we meet at the local sheriff's office and let him know we're in town. Okay?"

"Sure," Wilson said.

"Just a suggestion, of course," Clint kidded.

Clint and Wilson split up in front of the café where they had eaten, and Clint found his way to the telegraph office. He wrote down his message and handed it to the clerk, who scanned it to make sure he could read it.

"I'm staying at the hotel, when the reply comes in," Clint said. "If I'm not there you can just leave it at the desk."

"Yes, sir."

Clint couldn't help but comment, "This is a pretty small town to have a telegraph office."

"Folks around here are expecting us to grow."

"Why is that, exactly?"

"It's time," the clerk said.

"I mean, uh, what's the reason? Is there a mine hereabouts?"

"No."

"What about a big ranch?"

"Just some small ones."

"Then . . . how do you expect to grow?"

"A little at a time," the clerk said.

"Uh-huh," Clint said. "Well, bring that reply to the hotel."

"Yes, sir."

Clint didn't know who was behind bringing the telegraph to Buxton, but whoever it was, he wondered if they had done enough research before the decision had been made.

Clint reached the sheriff's office before Wilson but decided not to go in until the deputy had arrived. At that moment, however, the door opened and a man wearing a badge stepped out.

"Were you waiting to see me, friend? I'm Sheriff Bennett," the man said.

"Uh, well, I was, but I was waiting for a friend of mine, as well. We were going to see you together."

"I was just stepping out to get a bite to eat," the sheriff said. "Was it important?"

"Not so important it couldn't wait an hour or so."

"Well, good," the man said. He was in his fifties,

and he touched a stomach that seemed on the verge of bursting the buttons of his shirt. "If I don't eat regular my stomach lets me know about it. I'll be back in just over an hour. We can talk then, all right?"

"Suits me, Sheriff," Clint said. "One hour."

"Or a little more."

Clint nodded and said, "I'll remember."

As the sheriff walked away Clint noticed a wooden chair nearby. He walked over and sat in it to await Paul Wilson's arrival.

# TWENTY-THREE

"What are you doing?" Wilson asked when he got there and saw Clint sitting in the chair.

"Waiting."

"For me?"

"And for the sheriff. He was on his way out when I got here."

"Out where?"

"To lunch."

"And he couldn't wait?"

"Well," Clint said, "his hunger beckoned, and when you've got a stomach like his . . ."

"So are we just going to wait?"

"Do you have a better idea?"

"No."

"Did you find out anything?"

"No," the deputy said. "Nobody seems to have seen a family like the one I described."

Wilson looked around, as if seeking another chair. Resigned to the fact that there wasn't one, he sat down on the edge of the boardwalk.

"How could they have been here and not been seen?" he asked.

"Maybe they weren't here, then."

"And maybe they're not in California either."

Clint leaned forward in his chair.

"Do you want to go back, Paul?"

"I don't want to," Wilson said, "but who's watching things back there while I'm all the way in California?"

"I'm sure Frank is looking after things."

"How? He's laid up."

"He probably hired someone else as a deputy."

"Nobody in that town wants that job."

"So maybe they hired someone from out of town," Clint said. "I'll tell you what, why don't you go send him a telegram. Maybe he'll even tell you to come back."

"Probably not," Wilson said, but he stood up. "I'll send one, though, just to let him know where we are and what we've found."

"Meaning nothing."

"Exactly," Wilson said. "I'll meet you back here."

"Good," Clint said. "The sheriff should be back soon."

"If he comes back before me, I guess you could talk to him, huh?"

"Sure," Clint said, "I'll keep him entertained until you show up."

As Wilson walked away Clint wondered if Frank Dobbs would tell the young man to come back. If he did, Wilson would probably return, and what would he do then? Continue on with Newly? With no one with a badge accompanying them?

Dobbs wouldn't tell him that, though, not with that young girl's bullet hole still in him.

"I got back a little early," the sheriff said, drawing Clint's attention.

"Didn't mean to rush your lunch."

"I didn't rush," the man said. "I just finished early. Where's your friend?"

"He showed up, but he went to send a telegram."

"Well, do you want to come in and talk?"

"Sure," Clint said. "He'll be along."

Bennett opened the door and they both entered. The office looked much like every other sheriff's office Clint had ever been in. He wondered when, if ever, they would take on a different look.

"Why's this friend so important?" Bennett asked, seating himself behind his desk.

"He's the one with the badge," Clint said, sitting across from the man.

"A lawman?"

"A deputy," Clint said, "from Langdon, Arizona."

"Never heard of it," Bennett said. "What's a deputy from Langdon, Arizona, doing in California?"

"We're what's left of a posse trailing a gang of bank robbers."

"They musta done somethin' worse than just robbing a bank for you to trail them this long."

"They did," Clint said, "they shot and killed a female teller, and then shot the sheriff."

"What's his name?"

"Frank Dobbs."

Bennett thought a moment then said, "Don't know it. What might your name be?"

"Clint Adams."

The man's eyebrows went up, and he sat back in his chair.

"Now that name I know," he said. "Don't tell me you're a deputy, too."

"No," Clint said, "I'm just a friend of Frank Dobbs."

"I suppose you're thinkin' that this gang is headed my way?"

"We hope they were," Clint said. "Our best guess is they rode into California."

"They could stop at a lot of small border towns."

"I know it."

"Well," Bennett said with a sigh, "maybe you'd better tell me about it—until your friend gets back."

Clint went on to describe the gang to Bennett, who found the story very interesting.

"That's a new switch on robbin' banks," he said, when Clint finished. "Is it workin'?"

"It worked in Langdon," Clint said, "and I think that was their test case."

"But they shot a lawman, so they're tryin' to put some distance between them and you, right? Before they hit another bank?"

"That's what we think."

"Makes sense," Bennett said.

At that moment the door opened and Paul Wilson entered. Clint made the introductions, and the two lawmen shook hands.

"Has Clint filled you in, Sheriff?" Wilson asked.

"He has told me a very interesting story," Bennett said. "You're a little out of your jurisdiction, aren't you, son?"

Wilson bristled at being called "son."

"I guess I am," he said stiffly, "but my sheriff's been shot, and I aim to get the ones who done it."

"That's admirable, uh, Deputy. I didn't mean no offense. It's just that you're, well . . ."

"A little young?"

Bennett grinned and said, "Yeah, just a little, but I guess everybody's young once, huh?"

"I guess," Wilson said, still not completely mollified.

"Well," Bennett said, "I don't know what I can do to help you gents. If those bank robbers passed through here, they did it without me seein' them, and I don't see how that would be possible."

"No," Wilson said, "I don't either. I've been through your town, and it's not very big."

"Maybe not," Bennett said, "but folks around here have hopes of gettin' bigger. We got a telegraph office, you know."

"We know," Clint said, "we've made use of it." He decided not to ask the sheriff the same questions he'd asked the clerk at the telegraph office. He was afraid he'd get the same answers.

"Well," he said, standing up, "we just wanted to check in with you, Sheriff. There's three of us, and we'll be spending the night and getting an early start in the morning."

The sheriff stood, also.

"I'm sorry I couldn't be more help."

"You could be, if you've a mind to," Clint said.

"How's that?"

"I assume you know some of the lawmen in towns near here?"

"All of 'em."

"Maybe you could send them some telegrams, see if they know anything."

Bennett took off his hat so he could scratch his head, then replaced it. He didn't have a lot of hair on his head.

"Not all the towns have telegraph offices like we do," he said, "but some do. I could do that, I suppose. Might not have an answer before you leave, though."

"We could contact you when we get to the next town with a telegraph and see if you learned anything."

"Okay," Bennett said, "we'll do 'er. I don't mind

tryin' to help, 'specially when another lawman's been shot.''

"We appreciate that, Sheriff," Wilson said.

"Who's the other fella in town with you?" Bennett asked as they headed for the door.

"His name's Newly," Wilson said, opening the door, "and you probably wouldn't like him."

"Why's that?" Bennett asked.

"He's even younger than I am," Wilson said, and went out the door.

Clint simply shrugged at the sheriff, and followed.

Outside Wilson said, "What an ass."

"Oh, he's not so bad," Clint said. "You're just pissed because he called you 'son.' You're going to get that, you know."

"I know, I know . . ." Wilson said.

"Did you get through to Frank?"

"Sent the message," Wilson said. "I told the clerk to bring the reply to the hotel."

"We might as well go back there, then," Clint said, "since we're both waiting for answers."

"Why not?" Wilson asked. "It's as good a place as any to spend the time. Maybe Newly will be there."

"Just how much younger than you is he, anyway?" Clint asked.

Wilson blew some air out of his mouth and didn't answer.

# TWENTY-FOUR

Newly didn't show up at the hotel until after Clint and Wilson each received the replies to their telegrams.

Clint's came first: Rick Hartman still had no information on the gang who had robbed the bank in Langdon. He said he'd continue to keep his ears open, but it didn't look as if they had found their next bank yet.

"That figures," Wilson said.

Clint looked at the young man, who appeared to be very tired.

"How many times have you been out with a posse, Paul?" he asked.

"Countin' this one? Twice."

"You need to pace yourself," Clint said. "Turn in early tonight, and get some much needed rest. I'll wait here for Newly."

"What if Frank sends a telegram?"

"I'll take it, don't worry," Clint said. "I'll tell you what it says in the morning."

They were sitting in the lobby of the hotel together, no one else around except the clerk.

"Okay," Wilson said, "okay, I am kind of tired. I don't know how you do it, bein'—uh—"

"A lot older than you?"

"I didn't mean—"

"That's okay, Paul," Clint said, "I am a lot older than you, but I've spent most of my life in the saddle and sleeping on the ground. You'll get used to it."

"I hope so," Wilson said. "I want the law to be my life, Clint. I know that means I'll be ridin' with posses all my life."

"The law can be your career if you want it to be, Paul," Clint said to him, "but don't try to make it your life. There's a difference."

Paul Wilson nodded, said good night, and went up to his room.

A half an hour later the clerk appeared at the hotel again, this time with Wilson's reply from Frank Dobbs. Dobbs told Wilson not to worry about what was happening in Langdon, just get the job done no matter how long it took. Clint was starting to wonder if Wilson was ready for that kind of commitment.

About twenty minutes later Newly came walking into the lobby.

"Where've you been?" Clint asked. "We want to get an early start in the morning."

"I been around," the young man said.

"Are you drunk?"

"Naw," Newly said. "I don't drink that much. I like to know what's goin' on around me."

"That's a good attitude to have," Clint said. "What have you been doing?"

"Talkin' to people."

"Find out anything?"

"I might have," Newly said. "Seems there's a ranch

west of here. Hear the owner will let you stay there if you're runnin' from the law—for a price, of course.''

''Is that a fact?'' Clint asked. ''That's good to know, Newly. We can check that out on the way out of town tomorrow.''

''That's what I thought, Mr. Adams,'' Newly said. ''What's that you got?''

Clint looked down at the telegram in his hand.

''Telegram from Langdon.''

''Oh? How's the sheriff doin'?''

''Seems to be doing fine,'' Clint said. ''He wants the deputy to keep tracking the robbers and not worry about anything at home.''

''So we're goin' on, then?''

''We are,'' Clint said. ''You'd better get some rest.''

''It's funny.''

''What is?''

''You,'' Newly said. ''You're the oldest one of the three of us, and you seem to need the least rest.''

''Yeah,'' Clint said, ''that is funny, isn't it?''

# TWENTY-FIVE

"I got one picked out," Wilkins said. He looked around the room at their faces: Beth, Holly, Sally, and Ben.

"One what?" Ben asked.

"A bank, silly," Sally said. "He's got a bank picked out. Ain't that right, Stan?"

"That's right, Sally," Wilkins said, smiling at her. "You're a smart girl."

Ben pouted, but said nothing.

"Where is it?" Beth asked. "Here in town?"

"No," Wilkins said, "the next town over."

"How do you know about it?"

"Remember that ranch we stayed at, outside of that town? What was it?"

"Buxton," Ben said, trying to make points.

"Right," Wilkins said.

Ben pouted again, wondering how come he wasn't being told how smart he was.

"Buxton," Wilkins said. "That rancher told me about this bank that was ripe to be taken."

"And you took his word for it?"

"No," Wilkins said, "I didn't. I went and checked it out. That's where I've been all day."

Beth had wondered where he'd been all day long. She was going to have to take his word for it.

"So when do we do it?" she asked.

"Tomorrow."

"That soon?" Holly asked.

Beth looked at her.

"It can't be soon enough for me," she said, speaking to Wilkins but still looking at Holly. "I'm tired of having no money."

"We have money," Wilkins said, "but we're going to have more—a lot more."

"That sounds good to me," Ben said.

"Me, too," Sally said, drawing a dirty look from Ben.

"What about you, Holly?" Wilkins asked. "Are you ready to go?"

"Sure," she said, as they all looked at her, "if everyone else is."

"All right, then," Wilkins said. He took a piece of paper from his pocket and spread it out on the bed. "This is the layout of the bank. Gather around and take a look . . ."

They spent an hour going over the plan, and once again it was up to Holly to take care of the local sheriff.

After the briefing was over, Holly went to her room to wait for Wilkins. She knew he'd be coming, and she worked on phrasing what she had to say correctly, so as not to anger him.

Finally, she heard the doorknob turn and Wilkins entered her room.

"I swear," he said, "it takes Beth longer and longer

to fall asleep these days, but when she does she sleeps soundly.''

Holly was sitting on the bed, fully dressed.

"Did you get impatient?" he asked, sitting next to her.

"Yes . . ."

He tilted her chin up with his fingers and kissed her mouth. She kissed him back, trying to act interested.

"What's wrong?" he asked, sensing something.

"I, uh, just wanted to talk a little bit about tomorrow," she said.

"What about it?" he asked, running his hand up and down her arm. "Didn't you understand everything?"

"Oh, I understood perfectly," she said. "I was just wondering if you shouldn't give Sally the job of holding the sheriff?"

"And why is that?"

"She wants more to do," Holly said. "Don't you think she deserves a chance?"

"Well," Wilkins said, leaning back on his hands—which suited her, because then his hands weren't on her—"to tell you the truth, I don't have as much faith in her as I have in you. I don't trust her as much as I do you."

"Well," Holly said, "I think she should—"

"You know what?" Wilkins asked, cutting her off.

"What?"

He sat up again and ran his fingers along the line of her jaw.

"I think you're thinking too much, Holly," he said. "I think you should just do what I tell you to do, huh?"

"But—"

He took her jaw firmly in his hand and squeezed.

"No buts, all right?"

Thinking she had probably pushed him as far as she could, she said, "All right, Stan."

"Good girl," he said, releasing her jaw. "Now, why don't you get undressed? I want to watch."

"A-all right."

She stood up and started to undress. When she was naked he stared at her small, round, firm breasts and felt his penis hardening, thickening, lengthening. He reached out and touched her skin, her nipples, then pulled her to him so he could bury his face in her flesh. He sucked on her nipples and slid one hand down over her belly until he was rubbing her between her legs. She moaned and put her arms around him, but with his face buried in her breasts he did not see the look on her face, which was one of discomfort rather than desire.

And when he took her he turned her over and took her from behind, so she was free to express anything she liked with her face—except, as always, she hated herself for becoming aroused, for closing her eyes as he drove into her, making her wet, making her respond, reaching around and fondling her breasts. When they had sex her body betrayed her, because while she did not like the man, she did like sex, and he was good at it.

She wondered, though, when she would be able to get away from him, to make a life for herself, to find someone else to do this with, someone she both liked and respected.

Was there a man like that out there, anywhere, or were all men like Stan Wilkins?

# TWENTY-SIX

Clint, Wilson, and Newly rode up to the ranch Newly had heard about the next morning, having ridden out of town early. They had stopped only to have breakfast in the hotel dining room, which had opened early.

The ranch wasn't much to look at. The house appeared to be a two- or three-room house. The corral was in need of repair, as was the barn.

"Doesn't look like much," Wilson said.

"Looks almost deserted," Newly said.

"Maybe your information was wrong," the deputy said. "If he's charging people to hide here, he sure isn't putting the money into upkeep."

"Somebody's here," Clint said.

"How can you tell?" Newly asked. He started to search the ground. "Is there sign?"

"Yes," Clint said, "but not down there. Up there, on the roof."

Both Wilson and Newly looked at the roof and saw smoke coming from the chimney.

"Oh," Newly said, feeling foolish.

Wilson remained silent, trying to hide his feelings of foolishness.

"Let's ride up to the house," Clint said, "but be careful. If he's used to dealing with outlaws, then he's probably quick to show a gun, and maybe use it."

Newly started to take up his rifle but Clint stopped him.

"No," he said, "if it comes to that I'll handle it." He looked at Wilson. "That okay with you, Paul?"

"Sure," Wilson said. "You're the one who can use a gun the best."

"Okay," Clint said.

"Let's go," the deputy said.

They rode up to the house slowly and, sure enough, as Clint had predicted the front door opened and the first thing they saw was the barrel of a rifle, followed by the man who was holding it.

"Stop right there!" he said sharply. "State your business."

He was a tall, gangly man in his early sixties, wearing worn work clothes. His hair was gray, what was left of it, and he had a gray stubble of several days' growth. His cheek bulged with what was probably a plug of tobacco.

"You can put the gun up, friend," Wilson said. "My name's Paul Wilson. I'm a deputy sheriff."

"Deputy from where?"

"Arizona."

"What are you doin' here, then?"

"We're a posse," Wilson said, "tracking some bank robbers."

The man laughed derisively.

"A three-man posse?"

"That's right."

"Who might you be chasin', then?" the man asked. "Some durn fool who held up a bank hisself?"

"No," Wilson said, "he didn't do it himself. He had a woman and three children with him."

Now the man laughed aloud, revealing teeth that were both yellow and brown, from years of chewing tobacco. In fact, at that moment he let loose a glob that hit the ground with a resounding *splat.*

"If that don't beat all. A man usin' his family to rob a bank."

"We were wondering if you might have seen them come through here?" Clint asked.

The man switched his gaze to Clint.

"You a deputy, too?"

"No," Clint said, "just a volunteer. Did you see them?"

"Well, if I had I'd remember, wouldn't I?" the man asked.

"Does that mean no?"

"That's what it means, mister."

"You mind if we have a look around?"

"For what?"

Clint shrugged.

"Just so our trip out here won't be wasted."

The man thought it over for a few moments, and Clint thought he was going to decline, but then he shrugged and said, "Sure, go ahead, have a look. Ain't nothin' for you to find."

With that the man put up his rifle and stepped back into his house, closing the door behind him. Obviously, he didn't mean for them to be able to look in the house, just the barn and the outside.

"Do we need to get into the house?" Wilson asked.

"That depends on what we find outside."

"What do you expect to find?" Newly asked.

Clint looked at both of them.

"You remember that wheel mark I showed you? With the distinctive marking?"

"Oh, yeah," Newly said.

"That's what we're looking for. Let's split up. I'll take the barn."

"Okay," Wilson said, "I'll take the front."

"That leaves me the back, I guess."

"Don't sing out if you find anything," Clint said. "We'll gather back here and exchange information. We don't want that old man to know more than he has to. All right?"

They were all agreed, and went their separate ways.

# TWENTY-SEVEN

Clint dismounted and left Duke outside the stable so the the big horse wouldn't trod on any tracks. He needn't have bothered. That distinctive wheel mark was right there in plain sight, first outside the barn, and then inside. Apparently, the robbers had left the wagon inside, then driven out the back doors of the small, broken-down barn. Clint walked outside and watched as the tracks led away. It would give them something to follow for a while. It would also lift the spirits of Deputy Wilson, who had obviously been starting to worry about losing the trail.

Clint took a moment to look round the barn a little further. It became apparent that the man, woman, and children had stayed in the barn, and not in the house, probably just overnight. There was no fire, but there were signs that people had been there. One particular hastily prepared hay bed still bore the imprint of a body.

Clint went back outside and walked Duke over to

where he was to meet Wilson and Newly, in front of the house. The rancher had probably been watching from the window, because the front door opened and he stepped out. He was still carrying his rifle but casually now.

"Find anything?"

Clint looked at him.

"I think you knew I would," Clint said, "or you would have taken care to wipe away the tracks, and the signs of people inside the barn."

The man shook his head.

"That ain't my lookout," the man said. "People wanna be careless, that's their business."

"So you're not denying they were here?"

The man shrugged.

"How can I deny when they left sign behind?"

"Tell me about them, then."

"Any money in it?"

"Not now," Clint said, "but I'm sure there'll be a reward."

The rancher was thinking that over when both Wilson and Newly came riding over.

"Nothing," Wilson said, dismounting.

"I didn't find nothin' either," Newly said, remaining mounted.

"I did," Clint said. "There's sign of them in the barn, and the rancher here was just about to tell me something about them."

The man looked at Wilson.

"You're the one with the badge. Could there be a reward in this?"

"I'm sure the bank will be offering a reward," Wilson said. "Probably a percentage of the money they took."

A percentage, Clint thought, that might come to a hundred and fifty dollars or so, but the rancher didn't know that. His eyes lit up as he imagined how much money that might be.

"Let's have it, then," Clint said.

"Whataya wanna know?"

Clint looked at Wilson, indicating with that look that the young deputy should ask the questions.

"How many were there?" Wilson asked.

"Five," the man said, "a man, a woman, and three kids."

"How many boys and girls?"

"Two girls, and a boy."

"How old?"

The man rubbed his jaw.

"Hard to say. I think the kids was dressed younger than they was. I'll tell you one thing, though."

"What?"

"There's gonna be trouble between one of them young gals and the older one."

"About what?" Clint asked.

"About the man."

"How old is the man?" Clint asked, as suddenly he had taken over the questioning.

"I'd say mid-thirties."

"And the woman?"

"The same."

"Could the young gal you're talking about be eighteen?" Clint asked.

"She could," the man said. "Looked younger, but she could."

"Who was in charge?" Wilson asked.

"The man," the rancher said, "and I mean, he was *in charge*. Those other four, they did whatever he told them."

"Was he . . . rough with them?" Wilson asked.

"Whataya mean?"

"Did any of them look like they were being forced?" Clint asked.

"Forced? Naw, not forced, they just all . . . well, did what he said. I think they was all afraid of him, but none of them looked like they wanted to get away, or nothing."

"Do you know where they went?"

"Well . . ."

"Well what?" Clint asked.

"I ain't exactly sure where they went, but . . ."

"But what?"

The man suddenly looked sheepish and said, "I did sort of, uh, tell them about a bank I heard was ripe for pickin'. Of course, I heard *that* a couple of months ago. Could be somebody hit it already. Could be they'd run into some trouble if they tried." He rubbed his jaw again. "Guess I shoulda tole them that, too, huh?"

# TWENTY-EIGHT

Glenn Boyd, the manager of the Mesa Flats Bank, came out of his office and looked around. His newly instituted security measures were in place. After the bank was robbed two weeks ago he vowed never to let it happen again. To that end he placed one uniformed, armed guard inside the bank, and two other guards, one dressed like a customer, one dressed like a teller. With three armed guards inside, and one on the roof, he felt sure that the bank was safe.

When the door opened he saw a family of four walk in: a father, mother, and two children, a boy and a girl. There were half a dozen other customers in the bank, as well, and it seemed as if business was back to normal. As he turned to go back into his office, though, he heard someone say, "All right, this is a holdup, ladies and gents. If everyone does as they're told, no one will get hurt."

Boyd closed his eyes and thought, Oh, no, not again!

• • •

"Get the door, Sonny," Wilkins said to Ben, who nodded and moved to the door. He took up his position there, looking out the window, waiting for trouble.

"Mother, you and Sister watch these nice people."

"Yes, Father."

Wilkins looked at the armed guard.

"You want to go for that gun on your hip, son?" he asked.

The man didn't answer, but from the way he was flexing his hand it was clear that he did.

"I tell you what," Wilkins said, extending his gun hand so that his gun was pointed right at the man, "why don't you either go for it, or lift it out with two fingers and drop it to the floor."

He noticed the man's eyes go to another man who was standing across from him, as if for a signal.

"You. Are you the bank manager?" Wilkins asked Glenn Boyd.

"That's right," Boyd said, "and you are making a terrible mistake."

"This man is waiting for a signal from you," Wilkins said, indicating the guard. "Is he getting paid enough to die?"

Boyd, fuming, looked at the guard and said, "Drop your weapon to the floor, Mr. Case."

The guard lifted his gun out of his holster with two fingers and dropped it to the floor.

"Now," Wilkins said, "that's nice and cooperative. Let's keep it that way. Mr. Bank Manager?"

"Yes?"

"Would you join me behind the cages, please?"

Boyd moved behind the cages with the three tellers, and Wilkins followed him.

"Up against the wall, people," he told the three tellers, one man and two women. They obeyed immediately.

Wilkins inspected the cages and found a gun in one of them.

"Whose cage is this?" he asked.

"Mine," the man said. He was actually not a teller, but one of Boyd's undercover guards.

"Mind telling me why you have a gun behind your cage?" Wilkins asked, tucking the gun into his belt.

"Uh . . . we been robbed before."

"Is that so?" Wilkins asked. "Usually it's only the bank guard that has a gun, not the teller."

The man didn't reply.

"Come here," Wilkins said, crooking a finger at the man.

The man moved tentatively toward Wilkins.

"That's close enough. What's your name?"

"Ted Finn."

"Mr. Finn," Wilkins said, "I'm going to ask a question, and I hope you give me the right answer."

"I—I'll try."

"Good. Here it comes. Ready?"

"I—I'm ready."

"Are you a teller, or a guard, Mr. Finn?"

Finn's eyes went right to Boyd.

"Don't look at him, Mr. Finn," Wilkins said, "look at me."

Finn obeyed.

"I'll ask you again. Are you a teller, or are you actually a guard?"

Finn hesitated, then his shoulders slumped and he said, "I'm a guard."

"Uh-huh," Wilkins said, and then looked at Boyd. "Mr. Bank Manager, how many other guards are in this bank, dressed like tellers, or customers?"

Boyd didn't answer. His security measures did not

seem so tight now, but who expected a family of four to rob a bank?

Wilkins cocked the hammer in his gun and pressed the barrel to Ted Finn's forehead. The man closed his eyes and waited.

"Mr. Manager?"

"One," Boyd blurted, "there's one more guard."

Wilkins removed the gun from Finn's forehead.

"Back against the wall, Mr. Finn."

Finn obeyed.

"Mother, there's another guard in here."

"I heard, Father."

Wilkins looked at Boyd.

"I can't keep calling you Mr. Manager," he said. "What's your name?"

"Boyd."

"Mr. Boyd, this is already taking too long, so I haven't got much patience. Tell your other undercover guard to drop his weapon."

Boyd compressed his lips and wished he were brave enough to refuse.

"Mr. Carlyle, drop your weapon, please."

A man who had been standing near the window produced a weapon and dropped it to the floor. It was a small, easily concealed pistol.

"Kick it," Wilkins said, and the man complied.

"Now step back."

Again, the man obeyed.

"Finn," Wilkins said, "you're gonna act like a real teller now. Empty the money from the cages into a bag. There's a good lad."

Finn grabbed a bank bag and started to obey.

"Mr. Boyd," Wilkins said, "you're going to open the bank vault now."

"I can't—"

"Right now," Wilkins said. "Or I'll start shooting people, beginning with you. It's up to you."

Boyd started to grind his teeth as he turned the dial on the vault.

# TWENTY-NINE

Just for a moment Holly considered giving the gun to the sheriff and turning herself over to him. But what guarantee did she then have that the man would actually catch Stan Wilkins? Besides, did she really want Sally and Ben caught, too? She only wanted to get away from Wilkins, but this was neither the time nor the place to do that.

"Listen, little lady—" the lawman started. He was seated behind his desk with his hands in the air. His gun was on the floor halfway between them.

"Now, Sheriff," Holly said, her voice surprisingly calm and confident-sounding to her, "we're just supposed to stay here quietly, isn't that what I said?"

"But . . . you wouldn't really shoot me, would you?" he asked.

"I'm afraid I would, Sheriff," Holly said, "that is, if you give me no other choice."

"Well," the lawman said, "I wouldn't want to do that."

Holly thought about the other sheriff, the one in Langdon, that she had shot. Both he and this one were experienced men and had done what she told them. It wasn't that sheriff's fault that she'd had to shoot him. What was going to happen, she wondered, when she ran up against someone with less experience, someone who wouldn't believe her when she told him that she would shoot him? If a sheriff actually went for his gun she'd *have* to shoot him, and kill him. Once she did that she'd be a murderer, pure and simple. She had to get away from Wilkins before that happened.

She just had to.

Wilkins put Finn to work emptying the money from the vault. He got a kick out of having a guard do it.

"That's all of it," Finn said.

Wilkins looked at the two packed sacks of cash.

"No cash left?" Wilkins asked.

"No," Finn said, "just some papers, some stocks—"

"Not interested in those," Wilkins said. "All right, take the sacks around to the other side of the cage."

Finn did as he was told, dragging both sacks. Wilkins realized that he was going to have to carry the sacks, they were too heavy for Beth or the kids. Maybe he did need another adult male for this gang, he thought.

"Now everybody out from behind the cage and against the wall with everyone else, please."

The people from behind the cage complied, including Boyd, who was already planning even more stringent security measures for the bank—if he still had a job after this holdup.

Of course, there was still the guard on the roof with a rifle.

There was still a chance.

"All right, Mother, you and Sister keep these nice people covered while I get the sacks."

"Yes, Father."

"Are we clear, Sonny?" he asked Ben.

"Clear."

Wilkins holstered his gun and stooped to pick up the sacks, holding both by the necks so that his arms dangled. The very bottoms of the sacks dragged on the floor.

"All right, Sonny," he said. "Open the door and you go out first."

"Right, Father."

With that Ben opened the door and stepped outside.

When Holly heard the shot she said, "Oh, no."

"Sounds like something went wrong, little lady," the sheriff said.

There were more shots and the sheriff said, "Very wrong. Want to give me that—hey, no."

Holly cocked the hammer on the gun, and the sheriff put his hands up to ward off the bullet.

"Shit," she said. She ran across the room and, before the man knew what was happening, she clubbed him over the head with the gun, knocking him to the floor, unconscious. Then she fired one round into the ceiling and fled from the office.

Any hopes that Wilkins had been killed were dashed when he came riding up to the jail with two sacks dangling from his saddle.

"Come on!" he shouted.

She got mounted and rode after him, and Beth and Ben and . . . and where was Sally?

Oh, God, she thought, as she rode after them, where is Sally?

# THIRTY

"We're all upset by Sally's death," Wilkins said.

Actually, Beth wasn't so much upset about Sally's death as she was upset that it wasn't Holly who'd been killed.

"But really, how was I to know there was a guard on the roof?" Wilkins asked.

They were in a hotel room in a town not far from Mesa Flats. Wilkins thought it would be better to hole up in a town pretty near Mesa Flats. Who would suspect that a bank robbery gang would do that?

"After all," Wilkins said, placing a stack of money on the bed next to the others, "I did figure out that there were two undercover guards inside the bank. I should get some credit for that, shouldn't I?"

"I think you should," Ben said.

"Thank you, Ben."

Ben smiled. Without Sally around he was already getting more attention, so he wasn't particularly upset by her death either.

"I lost count again," Wilkins said, standing up. Some of the money was on the bed, and some of it was still in the sacks. There was a lot of it, he knew that much.

"Ben, Holly, I think you should go to your rooms," he said. "I'll be able to count if I'm not talking at the same time."

"But . . ." Holly said.

"But what, Holly?"

"What about Sally?"

"Sally's dead, dear," Beth said. "There's not much we can do for her now."

"I think Holly's more concerned about how we're going to replace Sally, aren't you, Holly?" Wilkins asked.

Holly looked at him and said, "Sure, Stan."

"See?" he said to Beth. "All right, Holly, we can talk about it another time. Right now I've got to get an accurate count of this money. You and Ben go to your rooms."

"Come on, Holly," Ben said, going to the door. "We have to let Stan count."

"Thanks, Ben."

"Sure, Stan."

Ben opened the door, let Holly go ahead of him, and then followed.

In the hall Holly asked Ben, "Aren't you upset about Sally getting killed?"

He shrugged.

"Not really."

"Why not?"

"Because she was a pain in the neck."

"And if we have to replace her," Holly said, "don't you think that person will be a pain in the neck?"

"Maybe not."

"Why not?"

"Because maybe the next one will be another boy."

They stopped at the door to his room, the one he was supposed to be sharing with Sally.

"What about me, Ben?" Holly asked. "Do you think I'm a pain in the neck?"

"If I did, Holly," he said, opening his door, "I sure wouldn't tell you."

"Why not?"

"Because," he said, entering his room, "you're sleeping with Stan. One word from you, and I'm out— and I don't want to be out."

"I wouldn't do that, Ben," she said.

"That's what you say, Holly," Ben said. "See you later."

He closed the door in her face. She walked down to her room, entered, closed the door behind her and sat on the bed. She wanted to cry, but she dared not. Wilkins might hear her, or might walk in on her, so she just sat there, stunned by the day's events.

She wondered what Wilkins would do if he found out that she hadn't shot the sheriff.

# THIRTY-ONE

"You're not upset about Sally getting killed, are you, Stan?" Beth asked when they were alone in the room.

"Just for the same reason Holly is," he said. "Now we have to replace her."

"I think she should be replaced with a boy," Beth said.

"You might be right, Beth," Wilkins said. He got on his knees by the bed to begin his counting again.

"There's a lot of money there," Beth said.

Wilkins looked at her.

"Yes, there is, Beth," he said. "I told you there would be a lot of money involved, didn't I? Even before we left the East, didn't I tell you that?"

"Yes, you did."

He spread his arms and said, "And look at it. It's not even all out of the sacks."

Beth came over and got on her knees next to him.

"Dump it all out, Stan," she said. "Dump it all out of the sacks."

He looked at her, then picked up the two sacks and upended them onto the bed. Some of the money was bound, and some of it was loose, and it made an impressive pile on the bed.

"Do you know what I want to do now, Stan?" Beth asked, standing up.

"No, what?"

He watched as she unbuttoned her shirt and removed it. Naked to the waist, she undid her pants and bent over to remove them. Her breasts swayed and bumped each other while she did this, and then she was naked.

"I want to roll around on it naked," she said.

"Okay."

"And then I want to make love on it."

Wilkins was surprised at how aroused he was becoming. As Beth got on the bed and began to roll around naked on the money, he stood up, pulled off his boots, and hastily removed the rest of his clothes. He stood there with a huge erection, watching her roll around, until she reached out, took hold of his penis, and drew him onto the bed with her.

"Fuck me," she said, pulling on him, "fuck me on the money, Stan!"

He pushed her down onto her back and straddled her. His penis felt bigger than it had ever felt before, even with Holly. He spread her legs and enjoyed the lascivious look on her face as he poked at her and entered her cleanly, easily, because she was so wet.

"Come on, my big bull," she said, pulling him down on top of her, wrapping her arms and legs around him, "fuck me hard . . . hard . . . harder . . . oh, harder . . ."

# THIRTY-TWO

It didn't take long after riding into Mesa Flats for Clint, Wilson, and Newly to hear about the bank robbery. In fact, the liveryman told them about it, and so did the desk clerk at the hotel.

"Second time in two weeks," the desk clerk said.

"Is that right?" Clint asked.

"And this time," he went on, "it was held up by kids."

"Kids?"

"Well," the man said, "a family. You know, a mother, father, and kids—and one of the kids got killed."

"What?" Wilson asked.

"That's right," the clerk said. "A little girl—well, she wasn't so little. The people in the bank said she was twelve or thirteen, but our undertaker says she was more like sixteen, maybe seventeen."

"And what about your sheriff?" Clint asked.

"The sheriff figures the other girl was probably that age, too, although she looked younger than that."

"Was he shot?" Clint asked.

"The undertaker?"

"No," Clint said patiently, "the sheriff, was he shot, too?"

"No," the clerk said, "but he was hit on the head."

"What's the sheriff's name?" Clint asked.

"Belford," the clerk said, "Sheriff Belford."

Clint looked at Wilson.

"We'll have to talk to him first," Clint said.

"Right."

"When was this robbery?" Clint asked the clerk.

"Yesterday."

"Let's put our stuff in the rooms and then go talk to the sheriff," Clint said to Wilson and Newly. "We're only a day behind them."

When they entered the sheriff's office they saw a man sitting behind the desk with a bandaged head and a sheriff's badge.

"Sheriff Belford?" Wilson asked.

"That's right," the sheriff said, with a look of misery on his face.

"My name is Paul Wilson, I'm a deputy sheriff from Langdon, Arizona. This is Newly, and that's Clint Adams."

The sheriff perked up when he heard Clint's name.

"Adams? What brings you here?"

"I think you'd better listen to this man, Sheriff," Clint said, indicating Wilson.

"What is it, Deputy?"

"We want to talk to you about the bank robbery yesterday."

"What about it?"

"We have some questions," Wilson said. "For instance, were you held at gunpoint by a young girl?''

''How did you know that?''

''They did the same thing to my sheriff,'' Wilson said, ''except she shot him.''

Belford sat up straight.

''She was gonna shoot me!'' he said. ''I'm sure of it. She cocked the hammer, and I knew I was a goner, but then all of a sudden something hit me. When I came to they were all gone—all except the other girl.''

''What happened with that girl?'' Clint asked.

''She was shot by a bank guard,'' Belford said. ''See, our bank was held up two weeks ago, and the manager decided to put on more guards. These robbers, they took care of the three guards inside the bank, but the one on the roof got by them.''

''And he shot the girl?''

''He says it was an accident,'' Belford said. ''He says he was trying to shoot the man who was carrying the money. He's all shook up about shooting a girl, even if she was armed and robbing the bank.''

''Can't rightly blame him for that, I guess,'' Clint said.

''What kind of parents take their kids to a bank robbery,'' Belford asked, ''and then leave one behind like that?''

''Well, Sheriff,'' Clint said, ''see, we don't believe that this is really a family. We think the adults are just using these kids to throw off the law, and the banks.''

''To catch them off balance,'' Wilson added.

''Well,'' Belford said, ''I gotta say she really caught me off balance. She walked in here sweet as you please and got the drop on me easy as pie.''

''You're lucky you're alive,'' Newly said. ''I wonder why she didn't kill you?''

''Damned if I know,'' Belford said. ''Like I said before, I knew she was going to, and then . . . nothing.''

"Is there a posse out looking for them?" Wilson asked.

"One of my deputies took one out this morning."

"Not yesterday?"

"It took a while for me to come to my senses yesterday," Belford said, "and nobody did anything while I was unconscious. By the time I knew what was going on, it was dark and too late. They went out first thing this morning."

"Why didn't you go with them?" Wilson asked.

"I tried," Belford said, "but I got dizzy and fell off my horse. Doc says I should keep my feet on the ground for a few days."

"Well," Clint said, "it might help you if we tell you what we know." He went on to explain about the wagon with the distinctive wheel.

"Much obliged," the sheriff said. "That'll probably come in handy."

"Do you mind if we take a look at the dead girl?" Clint asked.

"She's over at the undertaker's," Belford said. "I'll walk over with you, if you don't mind walking slow."

"No, Sheriff," Clint said, "we don't mind that at all."

# THIRTY-THREE

When they entered the undertaker's, the sheriff said to the ashen-faced man, "Let these men see the girl."

"Which girl, Sheriff?" the man asked.

"The girl that was killed in the robbery yesterday, Lester. Who do you think I mean?"

"Well," Lester the undertaker said, "I got other customers, Sheriff."

"You got another girl in here right now, Lester?" the sheriff asked.

"Uh, well, no . . ."

"Let these men see the girl, Lester."

"Yes, sir."

Lester led them to a room where he had the girl laid out on a table. The undertaker was a short man with a typical undertaker's pallor.

"There she is," he said.

"Okay, Lester," the sheriff said, "we'll take it from here."

"Yes, sir."

Lester left and the sheriff took a good look at the girl first.

"What are you looking for, Sheriff?" Clint asked.

"Sometimes, when Lester gets young girls in here— well, their buttons ain't always done up right, if you know what I mean."

"I think I do," Clint said.

"What's he do with them?" Newly asked.

Clint and the sheriff looked at him. Wilson just sort of looked away.

"He touches them," the sheriff said.

"Ain't he supposed to?" Newly asked. "I mean, ain't that how he gets 'em ready to be, ya know, buried?"

"He touches them in a different way," the sheriff said.

"Whataya mean?" Newly asked.

"Newly," Clint said, "we'll talk about it later, okay?"

"Sure," Newly said with a shrug, "I'm just askin'."

"Sheriff," Clint said, "can I examine her?"

"Examine her . . . how?"

"I want to check her pockets," Clint said. "Maybe I'll find something that will identify her."

"Oh, sure, go ahead," Belford said.

Clint went through the girl's pockets and found nothing.

"That's unusual," he said.

"What is?"

"Well, usually you find *something* in a person's pockets."

"Lester!" the sheriff called.

"Yes, sir?" The undertaker appeared in seconds.

"Bring me whatever you took out of this girl's pockets."

"I didn't take nothin'—"

"Just do it, Lester."

"Yes, sir."

He left and returned moments later with a few dollars and some small change.

"Is that all she had on her?" Clint asked.

"Well, there was some pieces of paper."

"What did you do with those?" Belford asked.

"I threw them out."

"Get 'em."

"They're in the garbage, Sher—"

"Get them out of the garbage, Lester!"

"Yes, sir."

He left and returned again, this time with a few slips of paper.

"What's written on them?" Wilson asked.

"Some doodling," Clint said. "Most of it I can't understand."

"Well, what can you understand?"

"A name. It looks like . . . Wilkins."

"First or last name?" Wilson asked.

"Last, it looks like. Appears she was doodling 'Mrs. Sally Wilkins.' "

"Could that be her name?" Newly asked.

"Well, Sally is probably her name, but . . . I've seen young girls doodle like this before . . ."

"Husbands," Belford said.

"What?" Newly asked.

"When a girl likes a man, she daydreams about being married to him," Belford said. "Sometimes, she'll even write her name down with his."

"So she's got a crush on a man named Wilkins?" Newly asked.

"That's how it looks," Clint said.

"Could he be—" Wilson said.

"That's what I'm thinking," Clint said. "He could be the man who's got them robbing banks."

"But . . . that rancher said they was scared of him," Newly said.

"She could be in love with a man and still be scared of him," Belford said.

"She could?" Newly asked.

"Yes," Clint said, "she could." He turned to Belford. "Thanks for your help, Sheriff. I don't think she has anything else that could be helpful."

Sheriff Belford walked them out of the undertaker's office.

"What do you boys plan to do now?" he asked.

"Well, we had planned to stay the night, but if we're only a day behind them that doesn't seem to make sense. Paul? What do you think?"

"I agree," Wilson said. "I think we should keep after them."

"They had to have stashed their wagon someplace nearby," Clint said. "Maybe another town. What's the nearest town, Sheriff?"

"Depends on the direction they went."

"Well, leave out east, because that's where we came from," Clint said.

So the sheriff named some towns north, south, and west of Mesa Flats.

"I guess we've got to pick a direction," Clint said.

"How do we do that?" Newly asked.

"We'll make an educated guess."

"The posse is still out there," Belford said, "and some of them are quick on the trigger. Stay alert or they might shoot you."

"Thanks for the advice. You know which way your posse went?"

"West, I think."

"Is there a tracker with them?"

"Naw," the sheriff said. "To tell you the truth, I

don't hold out much hope of them finding anything. They're just sort of . . . riding.''

"Okay," Clint said. "We'll go north or south.''

"Why?" Newly asked.

"Because it sounds as if this posse would pretty much have trampled any useful tracks by now.''

"I'm afraid you're right about that," Belford said. "I'd go with you boys, except—''

"Don't worry, Sheriff," Clint said. "We don't want you falling off your horse again.''

# THIRTY-FOUR

Holly looked up when Wilkins came into her hotel room.

"Come on," he said. "We're going for a walk."

"Where?"

"Just a walk," he said.

Frowning, she stood up and followed him out of the room.

Outside they turned left and started walking. The town they were in was so small it wouldn't take them long to get to the end of it. In fact, they were walking toward the livery.

"Where are we going?" she asked.

"I want to get the buckboard ready," Wilkins said.

"We're leaving?"

"Yes."

"Today?"

"Yes."

She didn't understand why he was bringing her along to prepare the buckboard.

"That's usually Ben's job."

"He'll be along," Wilkins said, "but I wanted to talk to you first."

"About what?"

He looked at her and didn't smile.

"Wait until we get there."

Well, getting there took all of two minutes and then they were inside the small barn.

"Holly," he said, "you didn't shoot that sheriff, did you?"

"W-what?"

"You heard me," Wilkins said. "You fired a shot, but you didn't kill him."

"I—I—"

"Don't lie to me," he said. "I can tell by the look on your face."

"I—I couldn't," she said. "I'm sorry, Stan, but—"

"Never mind," Wilkins said. "It's not important."

"It's not?"

"No," he said. "I've decided to change things a bit."

"Change? How?"

"Beth and I have . . . come to an understanding," he said.

"About what?"

"About us," Wilkins said, "about her and me."

"W-what about Ben and me?"

"When Beth and I leave," Wilkins said, "you'll be staying behind."

She couldn't believe her ears. This was what she had been hoping for.

"Ben and I?"

"No," Wilkins said, "just you. We'll need Ben."

"You're still going to rob banks?"

"Yes."

"W-will you be leaving me any money?"

"No."

She hadn't expected that. She'd thought that if and when he set her free he'd at least give her some money, but that was okay. It was worth it to get away from him.

"You don't seem very surprised," Wilkins said, "or disappointed."

"Oh, well, I, uh—"

"You never felt anything for me, did you?" he asked.

"Stan, I—"

"Don't deny it. You know, I was a fool about you for a while, Holly, but not anymore. Now I see you for what you really are."

"Stan, I don't under—"

"You don't have to understand, Holly," Wilkins said, putting his hands on her shoulders and holding her tightly, "you don't have to understand at all . . ."

As Wilkins was walking back to the hotel from the livery he saw Beth coming the other way. When they reached each other they stopped.

"Is it done?" she asked.

"Yes."

"Good," she said. "Good. It's about time. We were meant for each other, Stan."

"Yes," he said, "yes, we were. I'll get Ben and we'll get the buckboard ready. It's time to leave."

# THIRTY-FIVE

They took just enough time to buy some supplies, then retrieved their horses from the livery and left Mesa Flats. They rode straight out of town on the main road a ways, and then stopped.

"Which way would you go?" Wilson asked Clint.

"I'd go north."

"Why?"

"Because I wouldn't want to head for Mexico."

"Why not west?"

"I'd want to stay away from places like San Diego and Los Angeles," Clint said. "I'd head north and hit banks in some smaller towns, but mining towns, where there'd be payroll money."

"And not too much law," Wilson said.

"Right."

"Well, then," Newly said, "why don't we head north?"

"Why don't we?" Wilson said.

And they did.

They rode a ways and then Wilson asked, "Clint, what are we gonna do if they get rid of that wagon or buckboard they're drivin'? With the marked wheel?"

"Or if they get the wheel fixed?" Newly added.

"We'll just have to hope they don't."

"Seems to me a lot of this is bein' left to hope," Newly said.

"And chance," Clint said. "Don't forget that. You've got to be able to track, but you also need to be lucky, and so far we have. We just have to hope that our luck holds out."

"What if that posse catches them?" Newly asked.

"From what the sheriff said," Clint said, "that'd be the biggest stroke of luck of all."

"Any tracks?" Wilson asked Clint sometime later.

"A lot of tracks," Clint said, "but not our wagon."

"Too bad they didn't have a horse with a distinctive mark," Newly said.

"That would be a lot easier," Clint said.

"What if they're holed up in another town?" Newly asked. "One close by."

Clint looked at him.

"That would take guts," he said.

"Don't holdin' up banks take guts?" Newly asked.

"Yeah, it does," Clint said. "Newly, damn it, that's an idea."

"What is?"

"That they're in a small town somewhere, waiting for the posse to get tired of looking."

"There's lots of small towns," Wilson said. "We passed some road signs for some."

"I know," Clint said. "How about we double back and take a look?"

"At each town?" Wilson asked.

"We split up, we each check out a couple of towns, and we look for that wagon track."

"And when we find it?" Newly asked. "I know you could probably take them alone, but I don't think the deputy or I could." He looked at Wilson. "No offense."

"None taken," Wilson said.

"We'll arrange to meet," Clint said. "Whoever finds them can lead us back to that town."

"And if they ain't there no more?" Newly asked.

"They should be easy enough to track from that point on," Clint said. "Anybody got an argument against this?"

Both of the younger men shook their heads.

"Let's head back, then," Clint said. "We can start from those signposts."

# THIRTY-SIX

Clint rode into a town called Littletown, and it lived up to its name. It was very small, but it had a hotel and a saloon and a livery stable. Beyond that there were just a few buildings and a business or two. An ideal place to hide out, because who'd expect it? It was small, and too close to Mesa Flats.

Clint rode up to the livery and dismounted. It looked hardly large enough to house half a dozen horses, let alone a wagon or buckboard. He dropped Duke's reins to the ground.

"Anybody here?" he called.

No answer. He thought that the town looked so small they might be able to hear him at the other end.

"Hello?"

Still no reply. He walked up to the stable and looked inside. It appeared deserted. He entered and started looking around. The stalls looked as if they had been unused for months—except for two of them. He found some fresh horse droppings that were barely a day old.

He walked through the barn and out the other side. There was a small corral out back—or, at least, what used to be a corral. Two sides were completely gone, which would certainly limit its effectiveness. He walked up to it anyway, to check the ground, and the first thing he saw was that distinctive wheel mark.

The bank robbers had been here. They had probably come here directly from the robbery, itself.

Clint wondered if this town had any law. He turned and walked through the stable back to where he'd left Duke. He picked up his reins and started to lead him away, but Duke refused to budge.

"What's wrong?" Clint asked.

The big gelding tossed his head and flared his nostrils, blowing air out at the same time.

"You smell something I don't smell, Duke?" Clint asked.

Whatever it was the big horse smelled it kept him from wanting to move. It couldn't have been an animal, then, like a cougar or a bear. Duke would have reacted differently if it was something dangerous.

"Okay," Clint said, dropping the big gelding's reins, "I'll take another look around."

He went back into the stable, stood in the center and looked around, sniffing the air. That's when it came to him, too. He closed his eyes and inhaled. It was a stench he had smelled many times before, only it was faint. It would probably be a lot stronger in a few hours, but thanks to Duke he was aware of it now.

It was the smell of death.

# THIRTY-SEVEN

He found her underneath a pile of hay. He might not have seen her except one hand was exposed. Either she hadn't been covered completely, or an animal had unearthed her at some point. When he cleared the hay away he saw that she had not been gnawed at, so whoever had covered her had probably been in a hurry.

In death she was still very pretty, and looked to be eighteen or so, though she could have even been a little younger. She matched Frank Dobbs's description of the girl who shot him. He had no doubt that this was the second girl in the robbery gang. From the looks of it she had been strangled.

Although he had uncovered her, he did not move her. He went back out to where Duke was and patted the big gelding's neck.

"You were right, big fella," he said. "Now let's go and see if there's any law in this . . . town."

Further north, just outside of a town called Caspar, Stan Wilkins reined in the team pulling the buckboard.

"Why are we stopping?" Beth asked.

"I've decided it's time to get rid of the buckboard," Wilkins said. "Now that Sally and Holly are . . . gone, we don't need it."

"I still can't figure out what Holly was thinkin'," Ben said, "stayin' in that one-horse town."

"It was her choice to make, Ben," Wilkins said. "I gave her her share and that's that. Now there's just the three of us, but we can continue what we started, can't we?"

"We sure can," Ben said. "We don't need those . . . girls."

"No," Beth said, "we certainly don't."

She was amazed at how much sex on top of money had changed Stan Wilkins. The sex had been so much . . . better that she'd been able to convince him that all he needed was her. She'd actually talked him into killing Holly and leaving her behind. It was the first time she'd been able to exert any sort of control over Wilkins, rather than the other way around, and she liked it.

"We'll sell it here, and the team," Wilkins said, "and buy another couple of saddle horses, and then we'll be on our way."

"Suits me," Beth said.

"Me, too," Ben said.

Beth looked over at Ben and wondered if they needed him anymore either.

# THIRTY-EIGHT

"Nope," the bartender at the saloon said, "no law here. Closest is Sheriff Belford, over at—"

"I've been there," Clint said.

"Then I can't help ya," the grizzled old man said, "unless you want a beer?"

"Is it cold?"

The man closed one eye and stared at Clint.

"Never mind," Clint said, "I'll take it, as long as it's wet."

"It's wet," the man said. He draped the dirty rag he'd been mopping the bar with over his shoulder and drew Clint a mug of beer.

"Thanks." He sipped it and made a face. It was warm, but it was wet.

"What do you usually do when you have a dead body in town?" Clint asked.

"We don't have enough people livin' here ta worry about that kind of thing," the man said. "Why?"

"You've got a dead body now."

"Who?"

"A young girl."

"Where?"

"In the livery."

"My livery?" the man asked, aghast.

"You own the livery?"

"The livery, the hotel, the general store."

As far as Clint was concerned that was most of the buildings and the businesses in town.

"There was a buckboard out behind your place and two horses inside, probably up until yesterday. What do you know about them?"

The man closed one eye and stared at Clint.

"How do you know about them?"

"There are fresh droppings in two of the stalls, and wheel marks out back. Now, what do you know about them?"

"Wait a minute," the bartender said. "There was a young gal with them, and there ain't no young ones in this town. Is she dead?"

"She is."

"How?"

"Strangled."

"Who'd've done a thing like that?"

"The man who owned the buckboard, is my guess."

"They was up to no good," the man said, "I knew that when they came into town."

"What happened when they came in?"

"First thing they asked was if there was law here," the bartender said. "They was really happy when I said no. Course, they never asked if we had a mayor."

"And do you?"

"Yep."

"And that would be you?"

"Yep."

"Go on."

"Well, they asked who owned the livery and I tole them, and they said they wanted to leave their animals and buckboard there."

"And then what?"

"And then the fella said they needed three horses to rent."

"And did you have three horses to rent them?"

"I did."

"I didn't see any horses at the livery."

"I don't keep 'em there," the man said, "until it gets dark. I keep them behind the saloon, here, so's I can keep an eye on them."

"How many people live in this town?"

"I lose count," the man said. "Sometimes five, sometimes ten, somewhere in between mostly."

"And do you think one of them is going to steal your horses?"

"Ya never know."

"Okay," Clint said, "so you rented them the horses, and . . . ?"

"And they rode out. That was yesterday mornin'. They come ridin' back yesterday afternoon with one riderless horse."

"That was the other girl."

"Both girls got killed?"

Clint nodded.

"Who killed the first one?"

"A bank guard."

"A bank guard. Why?"

"They were robbing the bank in Mesa Flats at the time."

The old man's watery eyes popped.

"That family, they was bank robbers?"

"They were a gang," Clint said, "but now they're a threesome, because the two girls are dead. The guard killed one, and I'm sure the man who rented the horses from you killed the other one.''

"His own kin?''

"They're not really a family,'' Clint said. "They just wanted to look that way to hit a few banks. Actually, as far as I know they only hit two, but they made out very well in Mesa Flats. Maybe they've decided to stop.''

"You after them?''

"I am.''

"If they stop,'' the man asked, "how you gonna find them?''

"I'm going to trail them from here,'' Clint said, "following those wagon tracks as far as I can. Did they say anything about where they might be going?''

"Not to me,'' the man said. "We did our business, and they didn't talk to me after that.''

"Not even after they brought back the horses?''

"Nope,'' the man said. "They just left them in the livery and took their team and buckboard.''

"It is a buckboard I'm looking for, then?''

"Oh, yeah,'' the man said, "and they got some outfits on the back, sorry-lookin' saddles and such.''

Clint sipped some more of the beer and then put it down on the bar.

"What do I owe you for the beer?''

"Forget it,'' the bartender said. "Just catch up to that bastard. I got no use for a man what kills young girls.''

"You know what?'' Clint said. "Neither have I. Thanks for the help.''

"Wish I coulda tole ya more, friend,'' the bartender said.

"This is the closest I've been to them,'' Clint said. "I'm not about to let them get away from me now. Maybe you can do me one more favor.''

"What's that?''

"I'm riding with two other men, and I don't have time

to meet up with them. One of them's a deputy. If they come looking for me, will you tell them where I went?''

''Sure,'' the man said, ''if you tell me where you're goin'.''

''I'm going after that buckboard,'' Clint said. ''Just tell them where it was, and to follow the trail.''

''I'll tell 'em, mister,'' the bartender said, ''I sure enough will.''

# THIRTY-NINE

"Did you see this?"

"What?" Stan Wilkins asked.

The man he was trying to sell the buckboard to pointed to the rear left wheel of the buckboard.

"This wheel's got a cut in it, see?" the man said, bending and pointing.

"That doesn't weaken the wheel any," Wilkins argued.

The two men dickered while Beth and Ben looked on, and they finally agreed on a price not only for the buckboard, but for the team, as well.

"I'll be coming by a little later to look at some horses," Wilkins told the man.

"Be happy to sell you some, friend," the man said. "It's a good thing you ain't tryin' to hide from anybody."

"Oh?" Wilkins asked. "Why?"

"Look at that trail you left behind you," the man said.

"Why, with that mark in the wheel a blind man could follow it."

Wilkins looked at the ground and, sure enough, he saw that they had left a distinctive trail behind them.

"Yeah, you're right," he said to the liveryman, "good thing we ain't hiding."

He turned and walked over to where Beth and Ben were standing.

"What was that about?" Beth asked. "Why's he talking about hiding?"

"Come on," Wilkins said, grabbing her arm, "I don't want to talk about it here."

They walked away from the livery and headed for the saloon. Ben was trailing along behind them.

"Ben," Wilkins said.

"Yeah?"

"Here." Wilkins handed him a few dollars. "Go and buy yourself something. Meet us at the hotel a little later."

"All right!" Ben said. "Thanks."

Ben was very happy that he didn't have to vie for Stan Wilkins's attention with those two annoying girls anymore.

"What's going on?" Beth asked.

"We're not staying."

"I thought we were going to spend the night in the hotel?"

"No," Wilkins said.

"Is it because of that wheel?"

"I'm stupid!" Wilkins said, scolding himself. "I never noticed the tracks we were leaving with that wheel."

"But nobody's looking for us to be traveling by buckboard, Stan," Beth reasoned. "Nobody knows about it."

"I don't care," Wilkins said. "I just don't like the idea of leaving a trail like that behind us."

"So what are we going to do?"

"We're getting out of here, now. We'll go back to the livery right now and buy two horses."

"Two?" Beth asked.

"That's right," Wilkins said. "If anyone does trail us here, we'll leave them Ben. Maybe it will slow them down some having to deal with him."

"He won't put up much of a fight if a posse finds him," Beth said. "He'll tell all about us, especially if we leave him here. Why don't we just take care of him the same way you handled Holly?"

"When did you become so bloodthirsty?" Wilkins asked.

"When we got fifty thousand dollars out of that bank in Mesa Flats," Beth said. That was about ten times what they had expected to get out, and she didn't want to share it with anyone but Wilkins.

"No, we're not going to kill the boy," Wilkins said. "We'll just leave him behind. He won't be able to tell a posse anything."

"He can describe us."

"So can the people in those two banks we robbed," Wilkins said. "It won't matter. We're going to head north and keep on going until we reach Seattle—and maybe further."

"What's further?" Beth asked.

"Canada."

"Canada? I don't want to go to another country, Stan," she complained.

"Let's talk about that later," he said, turning her around and starting back to the livery, "after we get out of here."

# FORTY

Clint followed the wagon tracks to a town called Caspar—a real town this time, with an active population and more than one street. He didn't have to ride in far, though, as the tracks took him to the livery, which was on this side of town.

He dismounted and called out, "Hello?"

A man came out of the livery stable, and his eyes widened when he saw Duke.

"That's quite an animal, mister," he said. He was a mild-mannered looking man in his forties, with a fresh, open face. Clint thought that face must serve the man well when he was dickering for horses.

"Thanks."

"Looking to board him?"

"I'm looking for some information."

"About what?"

"A buckboard," Clint said, "with a very distinctive wheel marking."

The man stared at him for a few moments, then shook his head and said, "I knew something was wrong with those people."

"They were here?"

He nodded.

"A man, a woman, and a boy."

"What made you think something was wrong?"

"Just a feeling."

"They drove in in the buckboard?"

"Yep," the liveryman said, "and then I bought it."

"Bought it?" Clint asked. "You mean they're gone, and they left the buckboard here?"

"I'm afraid so."

"Can I see it?"

"Sure, come on in the back. My name's Raimy, by the way, George Raimy."

"Clint Adams."

If Raimy knew the name he hid it well.

"Well," Raimy said, "follow me, Mr. Adams, and I'll show you the buckboard."

They walked around behind the livery where the buckboard was nestled up against the back wall.

"Is it yours?" Raimy asked.

"No," Clint said. He walked around behind it and located the marked wheel.

"But it's stolen?"

"No."

"You mean . . . I don't have to give it back?"

"There's nobody to give it back to, as far as I know," Clint said.

"Then I don't understand what's going on," Raimy said. "Why were you tracking these people?"

Clint told the man about the two bank robberies, and the two dead girls.

"Well, that explains it."

"Explains what?" Clint asked.

"Why the man and woman left without the boy."

Clint's stomach turned cold.

"Is the boy dead?"

"No," Raimy said, "he's around town, someplace. He's sulking because they left without him."

"Well," Clint said, "they sure disbanded their little bank robbery gang quick."

"Just the two jobs?" Raimy asked.

Clint nodded and said, "But they did rather well on the second one."

"You still gonna go after them?"

"I am."

"Think the boy can tell you where they went?"

"I don't know," Clint said. "I guess I'll have to ask him, won't I?"

"Yeah," George Raimy said, "I guess you will."

Clint asked Raimy who the sheriff was in town. Raimy said it was a man named Fred Halloran. Clint got directions to the sheriff's office and walked Duke over there.

The sheriff was pouring himself a cup of coffee he'd prepared on a potbellied stove when Clint walked in.

"Help ya?" he asked.

"Sheriff, my name's Clint Adams and I've got a story to tell you."

"Is that a fact?" Halloran asked. He was a big, thickly built man, not fat, but he took up a lot of space in the room. "Well, then maybe you ought to do it over a cup of coffee, huh?"

"Coffee'd be good," Clint said.

Over the cup of coffee he told the sheriff everything that had happened since Langdon.

"To think I had that murderin' bastard in my town," Halloran said, when Clint finished.

"Not for long, according to your liveryman. Just long enough to drop the boy off."

"I know the boy you mean," Halloran said. "He's got no place to stay, and he's been walking the streets. Won't take help from anyone."

"Guess he doesn't trust anyone," Clint said, "not after the way he was treated."

"Maybe he'll trust you," Halloran said.

"Me? Why me?"

"You're after the people who left him here," Halloran said. "If you catch them you're gonna put them away, right?"

"Right."

Halloran shrugged.

"That might be reason enough for the boy to want to help you."

"You might be right, Sheriff."

Sheriff Halloran put his empty cup down on his desk and stood up.

"Come on," he said, "I'll help you find him."

# FORTY-ONE

They found Ben sitting on the boardwalk in front of the saloon.

"Hey, kid," Sheriff Halloran said.

Ben looked up at them. Clint judged him to be about fifteen, but he was small, and dressed the right way he could have probably passed for twelve.

"They won't let me in," he said. "They say I'm just a kid."

"Well, you are," Halloran said, "but I understand you're a kid who robs banks."

Ben looked startled, then tried to run, but Halloran clasped a big hand on the boy's shoulder, holding him in place before he could even get to his feet. The boy's shoulders slumped.

"This is Clint Adams, kid," Halloran said, "and he's come a long way to talk to you."

Ben gave Clint a long glance, looking both glum and defiant.

"I ain't gonna talk to him," Ben said.

"What's your name?" Clint asked.

"Ben," the boy said, before he could stop himself.

"Sheriff," Clint said, "I think you can take your hand off Ben's shoulder now. He knows he's got nowhere to run to."

Halloran hesitated, then released the boy, who flexed his shoulder.

"Ben, you want to go for a walk with me?" Clint asked him.

Ben shrugged.

"Are you gonna take me to jail?"

"Well," Clint said, "I guess that depends on you. I have come all the way from Langdon to find you, and there is a deputy sheriff right behind me. All I'll have to do is turn you over to him when he gets here, and you'll be off to jail."

Clint and Halloran exchanged a glance while the boy turned this over in his head.

"Or what?" he asked finally.

"Let's you and me go for that walk," Clint said. "We can talk about it some. Sheriff?"

"I'll be in the saloon," Halloran said, "if he takes off on you."

"He won't."

Clint waited until the sheriff went inside, then said to Ben, "Come on."

# FORTY-TWO

Ben got up and they started to walk slowly.

"Why'd they leave you behind, Ben?"

"I don't know," Ben said. "I can't figure it out."

"Well, at least you're alive."

"What's that mean?"

"Well, Sally's dead."

"She was shot by a guard."

"And Holly's dead."

Ben stopped short.

"What?"

"She's dead," Clint said. "She was strangled."

Ben frowned.

"You're lyin'," he said.

"It's easy enough to prove."

"Why would—"

"Why would . . . what?"

"Why would they do that?"

157

"Who are 'they,' Ben?" Clint asked. "What are their names?"

They started walking again, with Ben falling silent.

"They left you behind, Ben," Clint said, "and I think I know why. Want to hear?"

Ben shrugged.

"Do you know how much money they took from that last bank?"

"No," he said, "they didn't tell me—but they said it wasn't a lot."

"Over fifty thousand."

Ben stopped short again.

"Dollars?"

"That's right," Clint said. "I think that was a lot more than they thought, and certainly enough for them to consider not robbing any more banks—and if they weren't going to rob any more banks, they didn't need you and Holly anymore."

"But—"

"But what?"

"But . . . Holly and . . . and . . ."

"Go on, Ben," Clint said. "You can use their names."

"Holly and Stan, they were sleeping together."

"Stan Wilkins?"

Ben looked surprised.

"You know his name?"

"Just the last name," Clint said. "Sally had it written on a piece of paper."

Ben didn't say anything.

"What's the woman's name, Ben?" Clint asked. "The woman who played the mother?"

Ben hesitated, then said, "Elizabeth—Beth—Wentworth."

"Beth. Did Beth know about Holly and Stan?"

"I don't know."

"I'll bet she did," Clint said. "I'll bet she convinced Stan to get rid of Holly."

"She would," Ben said. "I mean, if she knew—I thought she'd kill Holly herself if she knew."

"So that leaves the question, why'd they leave you behind instead of killing you, too?"

Ben looked at Clint.

"Why?"

"To take the fall."

"What?"

"They were hoping that when we found you it would occupy us long enough for them to get away. They are on horseback now, right?"

"Right."

"Moving much faster than they had with the buckboard."

Ben nodded.

"Ben, I need to go after them. Stan shot that woman teller in the bank, right?"

"Right."

"And he killed Holly."

Ben didn't say anything.

"And Holly shot the sheriff, right?"

"Right."

"So what did you do, Ben?"

"I . . . watched the door."

"That's all?"

"That's it."

"Then I don't need to take you back with me, Ben," Clint said. "I just want Stan and Beth."

Clint put his hand on Ben's arm to stop their progress.

"Where'd they go, Ben?"

Ben looked up at him and Clint instinctively knew that the boy was going to tell the truth.

"I don't know."

"Ben—"

"I don't," he said. "They talked about hitting some more banks and maybe working our way to some of the mining towns up around Shasta."

"And then what?"

"Maybe San Francisco."

"Did they say San Francisco?"

"No," Ben said, "they said . . . north."

North, Clint thought, but how far? Oregon? Maybe Canada?

"I'll have to track them."

"Can I come?"

"Why?"

Ben flapped his arms helplessly at his sides.

"I . . . don't know anyone here. I'm alone. I . . ."

"The sheriff can look out for you, Ben."

"You said you wouldn't put me—"

"I didn't say he'd put you in jail," Clint said, "I said he'd look after you."

"I can't come with you?"

"No," Clint said, "you'd slow me down. When did they leave?"

"Earlier today."

"What?"

Clint thought they had left yesterday sometime. He was that close behind them.

"Come on," Clint said. "I'll leave you with the sheriff, and then I've got to get moving."

The boy dragged his feet some, but in the end he went along.

Clint went back to the livery to talk to the liveryman, George Raimy.

"The horses you sold them."

"What about them?"

"Were they good horses?"

"They were sound animals," Raimy said hurriedly,

but then he added, "but they weren't anything like your gelding. You should be able to catch up to them pretty easily in a day or so."

"I'll have to track them though," Clint said.

"That shouldn't be too hard, even if you ain't the greatest sign reader."

"Why not?"

"Well," Raimy said, rubbing the back of his neck, "I asked them if they wanted me to shoe the horses, but they were in too much of a hurry. They said they'd get it done another time."

"So the horses are unshod?"

Raimy nodded.

"Okay, I can track them—"

"There's one other thing."

"What's that?"

"Well," Raimy said, scratching his head, "I knew something was wrong with them, you know? I felt sure somebody was on their trail. I don't like dealin' with outlaws."

"What'd you do, Raimy?"

"Well, I . . . I took a file to the rear left hoof of one of the horses. Didn't hurt him, and it's not much, but that hoof is going to leave a print as easy to follow as that buckboard wheel."

"Good work, Raimy," Clint said with satisfaction, "real good work."

# FORTY-THREE

Clint picked up the trail immediately, thanks to the marking Raimy had put on the horse's hoof. As he rode he went over everything Ben had told him about the couple, Stan Wilkins and Elizabeth Wentworth. Apparently, there were from back East somewhere, where they made their living conning people out of their money. Ben had been impressed with that, and obviously still was.

"That's what I want to do when I get older," he'd said.

"Why?"

"Because it's more exciting than picking pockets."

"That's what you did for a living before they got you involved in robbing banks?"

"Yes."

"So why don't you want to rob banks for a living?"
Ben made a face.

162

"That's a little too exciting," he said. "People get killed."

Clint had known his share of people who made their living gaining other people's confidence. In fact, he numbered some of those people among his friends. That didn't, however, mean that he condoned what they did— which, by the way, was their business.

He stopped thinking about Ben and his future, and checked the ground to make sure he was still going in the right direction.

He camped that night, figuring that the next day he'd find their camp, and then he could figure how far behind them he was. Since he was on their trail and they probably didn't know it, he made sure he got enough rest. In the event that someone approached the camp, Duke would more than likely alert him. The gelding had saved his life several times before by sounding the alarm when danger was nearby.


"I hate this part," Beth said.

She meant having to camp out, cook over an open fire, and sleep on the ground, as opposed to being in a hotel.

"I kind of like it," Wilkins said.

"With the kind of money we're carrying around we shouldn't have to do this."

"We're between towns, Beth," Wilkins said, "and let's face it, we're still Easterners. We can't be riding around here at night. Why don't you try to get some sleep?"

"What about you?"

"I'm gonna sit up for a while, and keep watch."

"For what?"

"Just to be on the safe side."

"Well, all right. Good night, Stan." She kissed him shortly.

"Good night, Beth."

She rolled herself in her blanket and was asleep almost immediately. Stan looked at her. She had bitched all day about having to ride a horse, and was completely exhausted. The next day would be more of the same. In fact, every day would be more of the same, because she wanted to go back East, and he didn't. They could have split up, her going back East and him staying in the West, but she'd said she loved him. Besides, if they split up she'd want half the money.

He pulled the saddlebags with the money over to him and opened them. There was still a little left from the first robbery, and the whole fifty thousand from the second. He took out a stack and looked at it, then put it back and looked at her. He didn't understand how he had let her convince him to kill Holly. True, when they'd had sex on the money it had been great, but obviously it had screwed up his head, and she'd taken advantage of that—unfair advantage. He was a man who liked to stay in control, and he couldn't afford to let something like that happen again.

He closed the saddlebags and looked back over at Beth, sound asleep.

If he did it right, she'd never feel a thing.

The next morning Clint picked up their trail again and, sure enough, came upon the site where they'd camped the night before. The fire wasn't warm, but it had burned down by itself. Since they were Easterners they probably didn't know any better and hadn't bothered to kick the fire to death.

Half a day, he figured, that's how far behind he was, just half a day.

He stood up and looked around. Trees and grass, some

rocks and gullies. He found where they had staked the horses, and saw the distinctive mark George Raimy had filed into one horse's hoof.

He mounted up and gathered Duke's reins in, then thought he spotted something. There was a rock, big enough to hide behind, and he thought he saw someone behind it.

"Come on out," he said, "whoever you are." He was wary, in case whoever it was had a gun. Maybe the couple had had a falling-out and Wilkins had left her behind, too, like the boy. Maybe they'd come to a parting of the ways, but why would she stay behind without a horse? And had they split the money?

"Come on, I can't wait all day," Clint said. "Are you hungry?"

No answer.

Clint patted Duke's neck and said, "Come on, big boy, let's move closer, nice and slow."

He moved Duke closer to the rock and now could make out what appeared to be a foot, but he didn't like the angle at which it was resting. Whoever was behind the rock appeared to be lying down.

"Shit," he said, and moved Duke closer. When they reached the rock he dismounted, took a deep breath, and walked around it.

She was lying on her back, all right, eyes open and staring sightlessly at the sky. He bent over her and saw the marks on her neck. She'd been strangled by hand, rather than with a rope or something else. So that was how it was. With everyone else dead or left behind the man had decided to keep all the money for himself.

"Foolish woman," he said, shaking his head.

Three dead women. Clint wondered how the boy got so lucky.

He stood up and stared down at her. He didn't have time to bury her if he wanted to catch up to the man.

Maybe Wilson and Newly would come along and do it. Or maybe he could do it on the way back, if the animals hadn't gotten to her by then. Shit, the least the man could have done was cover her body with stones.

"Son of a bitch," Clint seethed. To strangle a woman while she slept. She had probably awakened, her eyes bulging, wondering what the hell was happening.

Clint wanted this bastard more and more, and as he mounted Duke he was determined to catch up to the man today.

# FORTY-FOUR

Stan Wilkins rode into Ardmore, California, leading a second horse. Little did he know that it was that horse which was leaving the trail behind that Clint Adams was following. He could have left the horse behind with Beth's body, or he could have set it free, but he chose to take it with him and sell it, even though he had fifty thousand dollars in his saddlebags.

He left the two horses at the livery, telling the man there that he wanted to sell the second. The man promised to look the horse over and decide if he wanted to make an offer on it.

Wilkins carried his saddlebags and his rifle to the hotel and checked in. He was tired, and he felt odd checking into a hotel alone for the first time in a long time. Maybe he'd buy himself some company tonight. It had been a long time since he'd been with a woman other than Beth— except for Holly, of course. Maybe the local whorehouse had a couple of young girls.

After he checked in he decided to go and get something to eat. He left the rifle behind in the room but carried the saddlebags full of money with him. He knew it would look odd walking the streets with them, but he decided looking odd was better than leaving them behind for some sneak thief to make off with.

He ate dinner in a nearby café, then went to the saloon and had a beer at the bar. He did not see the three men eyeing him from across the room.

"See?" Eddie Boggs said. "What did I tell you?"

"He does seem to be holding on to those saddlebags kind of tight, don't he?" Slim Tunny said.

"Wonder what's in 'em?" Del Ratlett said.

"Maybe we oughta find out," Tunny said. "Huh?"

Ratlett started to get up, but Tunny stopped him by putting his hand on his arm.

"Not here and now," he said. "Later. We'll pick a place."

Wilkins went back to the livery to talk to the livery-man about the horse.

"He seems sound," the man said. "I'll buy him from ya, but what's the business with the hoof?"

"Huh?"

"You marked him," the man said. "You do that instead of a brand?"

"I don't know what you're talking about."

"Lemme show ya."

They walked to the stall where the horse was, and the man lifted the leg so they could look at the hoof in question.

"I don't even know what it's supposed to be," he said, "but I noticed the mark in the ground. See?" He let the leg down. "Somebody could track you real good with that marking."

Wilkins's mind was whirling. First the mark on the wheel of the buckboard, and now this, and he hadn't noticed either time. Maybe Beth had been right. Maybe he should go back East, where this kind of thing didn't matter.

"I'll make you an offer on him, though," the man said.

"What? Oh, okay."

Wilkins let the horse go much cheaper than he might have, had his mind not been otherwise occupied.

Boggs, Ratlett, and Tunny watched as Wilkins came walking out of the livery with the saddlebags still over his shoulder.

"There's got to be somethin' good in there," Boggs said.

"Be patient," Tunny said. "We'll find out soon enough."

# FORTY-FIVE

Clint rode into Ardmore about three hours after Wilkins did. He had closed the gap between them by pushing Duke hard, and had been pleased when the tracks led to a town. With any luck, Wilkins was still in Ardmore.

He rode directly to the livery and saw the tracks from the marked hoof out in front and leading inside.

"Help you, friend?" The liveryman had come outside and saw Clint there. He was in his thirties, short and stocky with the scarred hands of a man who had been around horses' gnashing teeth for years.

Clint dismounted and faced the man.

"I'm looking for the horse that made those marks," he said, pointing to the ground.

The man looked down, and then back at Clint.

"Was it stolen?" he asked. "I didn't know it was stolen."

"It wasn't stolen."

"Well," the man said, "I just bought it a little while ago."

"How long ago?"

"Made the deal—oh, about twenty minutes ago."

"Twenty minutes?" Clint couldn't believe his luck. "Then the man you bought it from is still here?"

"Still in town, yeah."

"Where'd he go?"

"I don't know," the man said. "Maybe the hotel. He's a strange man."

"How so?"

"He carries his saddlebags with him everyplace he goes," the liveryman said. "That's kind of foolish, if you ask me. Tells people he's got something inside that means a lot to him. Some people might think he's got something valuable."

"Describe this man to me."

The other man did so and the description matched the one Ben had given him.

"Okay, thanks."

"This man," the liveryman asked, "is he in trouble?"

"He's in a lot of trouble when I catch up to him," Clint said.

"Then you'd better hurry."

"Why's that?"

"Because three men followed him when he left here," the man said. "I saw them across the way."

"You know these three men?"

"Uh-huh. They're bad. They're gonna rob him, I know it."

"And you didn't warn him?"

"I didn't have a chance," the other man said. "Besides, they would have killed me."

"This town got a sheriff?"

"Sure, Sheriff Tyler."

"Get him," Clint said. "Tell him what we talked about, and tell him to find those men."

"Uh, okay. You want me to take your horse?"

"I'll leave him here for now," Clint said. "Take care of him when you get back, but get to the sheriff first!"

"All right," the man said, "I will. Should I, uh, tell him your name?"

"Yes," Clint said, "tell him Clint Adams, and tell him I'm here ahead of a posse I was riding with."

"Clint Adams . . ." the man repeated in hushed tones.

"Go!"

The man ran.

Clint left Duke inside the livery and walked toward the center of town.

Stan Wilkins started back to his hotel from the livery but then decided to see if the town had a whorehouse. He walked around some, but if they had one it wasn't evident. He was going to have to ask someone, and there was no one better to answer that question than a bartender.

He went into the first saloon he saw, a smaller one than he'd been in before, and went to the bar.

"A beer."

The bartender stared at him.

"Hello?" Wilkins said. "I'd like a beer, please."

"You better go someplace else, friend."

"Why's that?"

" 'Cause you're a stranger," the bartender said. "They don't like strangers in here."

Wilkins looked around, didn't see anyone, and turned back to the bartender.

"There's nobody here."

"That's because we don't let strangers in here," the man said. He spoke slowly, as if he were speaking to a child. "The regulars will be here soon, and they don't like strangers."

"Well," Wilkins said, "I'll just have one beer and be on my way."

The bartender stared at him, then shrugged and said, "Your funeral," and served him a beer.

At that point the batwing doors swung in and Boggs, Ratlett, and Tunny walked in. They looked around and saw with great satisfaction that the place was empty.

"Better drink it fast," the bartender said, and then disappeared into the back room.

# FORTY-SIX

Wilkins turned and saw the three men standing inside the doors.

"Can I help you fellows?"

"What's in the saddlebags, friend?" Tunny said.

Wilkins's stomach went cold.

"W-what?"

"The saddlebags," Ratlett said. "He asked what's in them?"

"Uh, just some personal things."

"Personal things that you carry with you everywhere you go?" Boggs asked.

"Well, you know," Wilkins said, "you can't always leave things in your hotel room."

"Open them up," Tunny said.

"W-what?"

"Open them," Boggs said.

"You deaf?" Ratlett asked.

Wilkins didn't know what to do. He was wearing a

gun, but he was no good with one. He could stick it in a bank manager's face, or shoot a teller, but there was no way he could outdraw three men.

"You got another choice," Tunny said.

"What's that?"

"Put the saddlebags on the bar, and walk out."

"I—I can't do that."

"Then open them."

"I can't do that either."

"Then go for your gun," Ratlett said.

"You'd shoot me down for these saddlebags, not knowing what's in them?"

Tunny smiled and said, "In a heartbeat."

Wilkins couldn't believe it. How did he end up like this? What had he done to deserve this?


Clint saw a man wearing a badge coming toward him quickly.

"You the feller lookin' for trouble?" he asked.

"I'm not looking for trouble, Sheriff," Clint said, "I'm trying to stop it."

"Adams, right?"

"That's right."

"You with a posse?" The sheriff was in his fifties, tall and slender, fit-looking. Clint wondered how many sheriffs he'd met since this started, in so many sizes and shapes.

"I was. I'm ahead of them now, but our man is here in town. I heard he's being stalked by three other men—"

"Sheriff!"

They both turned and saw a man wearing an apron coming toward them. Obviously, he was a bartender.

"Trouble at my place, Sheriff," he said. "You gotta come."

"What is it, Al?"

"Tunny and his men, they're gonna gun down a stranger."

"This stranger have saddlebags with him?" Clint asked.

"That's the one."

"Let's go," the sheriff said.

They were running up the street when they heard the shots.

The sheriff hit the batwing doors with Clint right behind him. They both saw three men standing over a fourth, who was lying on the floor leaking blood from several holes. One of the men was in the act of picking up the saddlebags. He did so upside down, and some stacks of money fell out onto the floor, and onto the fallen man's chest.

"Tunny!" the sheriff yelled. "Put it down."

Tunny turned, saw the sheriff and the other man, and went for his gun. Boggs and Ratlett were still holding their guns, but they had to bring them to bear on Clint and the sheriff.

Clint drew and fired quickly, hitting both men before they could bring their guns around. The sheriff drew his gun and fired at Tunny at the same time the man fired his gun. The sheriff's bullet hit Tunny in the chest, while Tunny's tugged at the sheriff's shirtsleeve, drawing blood but doing little damage.

"Well," the sheriff said, "we did that like we been doin' it all our lives."

"Instincts," Clint said.

Clint and the sheriff now approached all four fallen men. Tunny, Ratlett, and Boggs were dead of single shots. The irony was that Wilkins—and Clint could see that this man matched the description—was dying from three wounds, but was still bleeding. The stack of money on his chest was soaking up some blood.

"Wha—" he said, pain etched on his face, confusion in his eyes.

"Wilkins?" Clint asked.

"Yes, bu—wha—why did this happen? What . . . did I do . . . to deserve this?"

Clint looked down at the man and said, "I'd tell you, but you don't look like you have the . . . time."

By the time Clint got the last word out, Wilkins was dead.

# EPILOGUE

Clint stared down at the naked girl in his bed. Blond, pale, sweet-smelling and even sweeter-tasting, she had made his two days in Langdon . . . well, sweet.

Her name was Annie. She was a short girl with big breasts, in her late twenties. She had the kind of body that would probably start to go to fat when she hit thirty, fleshy and comfortable. She had used her big breasts on him last night, rolling his penis between them until he was ready to explode, and then hungrily taking him in her mouth and sucking him dry. She had one of the most talented mouths he'd ever encountered, too, and she loved using it. She'd put her tongue in some places he'd never felt a woman's tongue before, and he had tried to return the favor.

He stared down at her naked butt now, full and firm and pear-shaped. He leaned over, ran his tongue along the cleft between her cheeks, then planted a kiss on each one.

"Are those good-bye kisses?" she asked.

"I'm afraid so, Annie," he said. "I'm leaving this morning."

She rolled over and smiled up at him. Her big breasts were flattened out on her chest.

"Kiss me here," she said, pointing to her right nipple.

He did.

"And here," she said, pointing to her left nipple.

He complied.

"And here," she said, pointing to her mouth.

He kissed her there, too, and it went on longer than he intended.

"And now here," she said, pointing between her legs.

"No, not there," he said, moving toward the door. "You taste too good, and I'd never get out of here."

"You chicken," she shouted, throwing a pillow at him.

"Bye, Annie."

"Good-bye, you beautiful man!" she called out as he closed the door.


He was walking through the lobby when Sheriff Frank Dobbs entered.

"Glad I caught you," Dobbs said. Behind him Paul Wilson also entered. Wilson and Newly had caught up to him in Ardmore, after Wilkins was dead. They'd been mad for a while at being left behind, but they got over it.

"I wouldn't have left without saying good-bye," Clint said.

"I have something for you." Dobbs handed him an envelope.

"What is it?"

"A reward from the bank—a small one."

"I don't need this, Frank," Clint said. "That other

bank paid me pretty well for recovering their fifty thousand.''

And he had split the money with Wilson and Newly.

"Well, this bank wanted to give you something, too.''

"Give it to Paul and Newly,'' Clint said. "They deserve it.''

"You got Wilkins,'' Wilson said.

"We tracked him together, Paul,'' Clint said. "You're going to make a fine lawman.''

Wilson beamed and Dobbs said, "So's Newly, I think. I deputized him this morning.''

"That's good,'' Clint said.

"Sure you don't want this?'' Dobbs asked.

"Give it to your underpaid deputies.''

"From an underpaid sheriff,'' Dobbs said, handing it back to Wilson. "Were you leaving?'' he asked Clint.

"I was going to have breakfast first. Join me?''

"Sure,'' Dobbs said.

"I've got rounds,'' Wilson said. "I'll say good-bye now.''

Clint shook hands with the young man and watched him leave.

"How are you feeling?'' he asked Dobbs.

"Fit,'' he said, "as long as it doesn't rain. Where are you headed?''

"I don't know,'' Clint said. "Probably someplace where there are no banks to rob.''

"Can't blame you for that, Clint,'' Dobbs said, as they left the hotel, "can't blame you at all.''

Watch for

**THE COUNTERFEIT CLERGYMAN**

196th novel in the exciting GUNSMITH series
from Jove

*Coming in May!*

# J. R. ROBERTS

# THE GUNSMITH